SCOTTISH WRITERS

Editor

DAVID DAICHES

This is a revision and elaboration of Thomas Crawford's widely acclaimed 1965 study of Scott. All aspects of Scott's work as a poet, balladist and novelist are examined with lively critical insight in the light of both Mr. Crawford's own perceptions and of the many recent studies of Scott that have marked the modern revival of interest in the man and his work. Mr. Crawford comes to grips with the underlying intention and themes in the novels and demonstrates how these are developed in individual works and how they relate to Scott's presentation of action and characters. There is a particularly searching examination of *The Heart of Midlothian*, which Mr. Crawford regards as Scott's masterpiece.

SCOTT

THOMAS CRAWFORD

SCOTTISH ACADEMIC PRESS

EDINBURGH

Published by
Scottish Academic Press Ltd
33 Montgomery Street, Edinburgh EH7 5JX

First published 1982
SBN 7073 0305 2

© 1982 Text and Bibliography
Thomas Crawford

Printed in Great Britain by
Clark Constable Ltd.,
Hopetoun Street, Edinburgh

CONTENTS

ACKNOWLEDGMENT

The Scottish Academic Press acknowledges the financial
assistance of the Scottish Arts Council in the publication
of this volume.

ABBREVIATED TITLES USED
IN REFERENCES

I. WALTER SCOTT
Except where otherwise stated, references to Scott's works
are to the Dryburgh edn., London 1892–5

A.	=	*The Antiquary.*
H.M.	=	*The Heart of Midlothian.*
I.	=	*Ivanhoe.*
K.	=	*Kenilworth.*
L.L.M.	=	*The Lay of the Last Minstrel.*
M.	=	*The Monastery.*
Minstrelsy	=	*The Minstrelsy of the Scottish Border*, ed. T. F. Henderson, 1932.
M.P.W.	=	*Miscellaneous Prose Works*, 1848.
O.M.	=	*Old Mortality.*
P.	=	*The Pirate.*
P.W.	=	*Poetical Works.*
R.	=	*Redgauntlet.*
W.	=	*Woodstock.*
Wav.	=	*Waverley.*

II. OTHERS

Child	=	F. J. Child, *The English and Scottish Popular Ballads.*
Craig	=	D. Craig, *Scottish Literature and the Scottish People 1680–1830.*
Cregeen	=	E. Cregeen, "The Cnanging Role of the House of Argyll in the Scottish Highlands", in *Scotland in the Age of Improvement*, ed. N. Phillipson and R. Mitchison. Edinburgh, 1970.
Grierson	=	H. J. C. Grierson, *Sir Walter Scott, Bart.*
Harry	=	K. W. Harry, "The Sources and Treatment of Traditional Ballad Texts in Sir Walter Scott's 'Minstrelsy of the Scottish Border' and Robert Jamieson's 'Popular Ballads and Songs'," unpublished Ph.D. thesis, University of Aberdeen. 2 vols., 1975.
Johnson	=	E. Johnson, *Sir Walter Scott: the Great Unknown.*
Lockhart	=	J. G. Lockhart, *The Life of Sir Walter Scott.*
Lukács	=	G. Lukács, *The Historical Novel.*
Welsh	=	A. Welsh, *The Hero of the Waverley Novels.*

FOREWORD

The first edition of this book was published in 1965 in Oliver and Boyd's Writers and Critics series. Though short and highly condensed it had a certain influence at the time, particularly (so I have been told) on young researchers. P. D. Garside, for instance, saw in it one of the signs "of a new readiness to take the suggestion of 'philosophical' origins [for Scott's historicism] seriously" ("Scott and the philosophical historians", *Journal of the History of Ideas* XXXVI, 1975, p. 497), and it has apparently stimulated some recent work on Scott as a poet. Its main lines remain the same, and I am surprised that I have wanted to change so little. A slight shift of emphasis in Chapter II as well as some additional details have been made necessary by Keith Harry's meticulous dissertation, which I had the honour to supervise (see list of abbreviated titles), and I have added to Chapter III to take note of discussions of *The Lay of the Last Minstrel* and *Marmion* by J. H. Alexander and John Pikoulis.

Despite recent attempts to downgrade *The Heart of Midlothian*, I still think it Scott's masterpiece. I have been much strengthened in this opinion by the remark of a "common reader", a devotee of Jane Austen, Henry James, George Eliot and Joseph Conrad, whose judgment of novels and novelists I trust more than that of any professional critic I know. After hearing one of those "Desert Island Discs" radio programmes where a celebrity is asked to name a single book besides the Bible and Shakespeare which he would wish saved from the wreck, she said: "for me, it would have to be either *War and Peace* or *The Heart of Midlothian*". The one work of British fiction fit to be put beside Tolstoy? It is at least a position which can be seriously defended.

Since the first edition I have modified my view of the last third of *The Heart of Midlothian*, which I now rate more highly than before. Critics as different as Northrop Frye and Raymond Williams have helped me here, but the greatest stimulus has been Eric Cregeen's purely historical account of the house of Argyll in the seventeenth and eighteenth centuries (see list of abbreviated titles), which makes it possible to measure Scott's social symbolism against the reality it both represents and explores.

The last chapter has been almost entirely rewritten, though the heading is the same, and the bibliography has been completely revised. I take pleasure in repeating my acknowledgements to the Carnegie Trust for the Universities of Scotland, who made it possible for me to work on the first edition so many years ago.

T.C.

CHAPTER I

LIFE AND WORKS

Scott's reputation with creative writers has never recovered from that decline which almost always sets in after the death of a major author. With Stendhal, indeed, the *volte face* took place during Scott's lifetime: up to 1825 he was enthusiastic, but in 1830—the year when he found his own distinct voice as a novelist—he suffered a violent revulsion, which soon hardened into a permanent attitude.[1] Balzac, however, was different. In the preface to the *Comédie humaine* he stated that his own fictional analysis of early nineteenth-century society stems directly from Scott: what Sir Walter did for the past, Balzac attempted for the present or near present, more systematically and perhaps in greater depth.[2] A whole school of historians grew up in his shadow, both at home and on the continent, and he provided both subject-matter and inspiration to generations of painters, illustrators and operatic composers.[3] Nor was his influence on the English novel confined to such romantic entertainers as Harrison Ainsworth or Bulwer Lytton. In their treatment of working-class and peasant characters, their use of romance themes and regional dialect, and even in their presentation of society, Dickens, the Brontes, Thackeray, Hardy, Elizabeth Gaskell and George Eliot were each in their several ways immensely in his debt. Ordinary readers, not just in Britain and America but all over Europe, remained faithful till about the turn of the century, though their favourites tended to be such medieval or Tudor-Stuart romances as *Ivanhoe* and *Kenilworth* rather than the far more significant Scottish

novels; but since then the decline has been rapid and
progressive. About twenty-five years ago, it is true,
professional critics and scholars began to take him up with
a new seriousness and even passion,[4] and a number of
excellent books of both general and specialist appeal were
published around the bicentennial of 1971. As we enter
the nineteen-eighties a new generation of Scott scholars is
making its presence felt, with fresh approaches and new
insights. But the latest contributions tend to be in the form
of minute examinations of particular works, or else they
approach the whole corpus with a selective thesis to be
proved; the broad overview is hard to find. It is the aim of
the present study in its revised form to present the
common reader and the beginning student with such a
general account, and to stimulate serious interest, both
inside and outside Scotland, in a writer who—as is
claimed in the last chapter—is still relevant to the modern
world.

Scott's work arose out of a conflict between two traditions, family and national, in a period of Scottish history
when both gentlemen and people had either to give way
before the power of money, or allow themselves to be re-
made by it, for better or worse. From his father, an Edinburgh solicitor or "Writer to the Signet," he got his
practicality, his habits of sober calculation and diligent
labour, his attachment to the Hanoverian establishment
and therefore, in the last resort, to Anglicisation; from his
mother came his obsession with the tales and legends of a
heroic past, including stories connected with his father's
ultimate ancestors, the Scotts of Buccleuch. Before his
second birthday, in 1773, he fell victim to a form of
poliomyelitis that left him lame for life. In order to
recuperate he was sent off to his grandfather's farm at
Sandyknowe, some forty miles from the capital, where he
made contact with the strongest of all the formative
elements that were later to mould his work—the oral
tradition of the Borders, and, beyond that, of Scotland as a

whole. From the shepherds he heard folk-tales and legends; from his grandmother, stories of the old days of the reivers and freebooters; from his uncle, eye-witness accounts of the Forty-Five and its aftermath; from servants and labourers, the songs and ballads that were still alive on the lips of the people. In later life he was to draw on popular literature of all kinds—broadside ballads, chapbooks, and published songs: but his first introduction to such material was *oral* and he never lost the sense of popular tradition as being not simply a matter of documents shut up in dusty archives, but rather a living record on the lips of successive generations. Many have claimed that there is a fundamental contradiction between Scott's romantic attachment to the past and his prosaic respect for the Hanoverian regime. Yet there are two things that should not be forgotten here—first, that his Toryism belonged just as much to the ultilitarian present as to his dreams of Jacobite and feudal glories, and second, that because of the folk sources on which it fed, his love of "old, forgotten, far-off things" had its democratic as well as its conservative side.

In 1778 he began attending the High School in Edinburgh, where he first met with the rudiments of that classical, Anglicised, cosmopolitan, yet in some ways still obscurely national culture which was the distinctive creation of the upper classes in eighteenth-century Scotland. Between his thirteenth and fifteenth years, he attended classes at Edinburgh University, only to be suddenly stricken with an internal haemorrhage that kept him in bed for many weeks.[5] He whiled away the time by omniverous reading in the literature of fantasy and romance. The folk culture which he had absorbed at Sandyknowe began to coalesce with his sick-bed daydreams, with orally transmitted stories about his own Border ancestors, and above all with the written account left by one of his forbears, Minstrel Scott of Satchells, who published in 1688, in verse, *A True History of Several honour-*

able Families of the Right Honourable Name of Scott. To Walter,
the entire history of the Borders seemed but a heroic projection of the epic deeds of the clan Scott, and at first he
viewed the history of the whole Scottish nation as simply
an extension of Border history and therefore of the annals
of his own family.[6] Thus the most vital experiences of his
first sixteen years came together in an imaginative synthesis of the aristocratic and the folk, the epical and the
romantic; and he had already established a reputation
amongst his schoolfellows as a born storyteller.

In 1786 he entered his father's office as an apprentice
Writer to the Signet. Here he was exposed to the bourgeois
side of his inheritance—to money values, worldly
ambition and sober calculation. The first step upwards
was taken in 1788 when it was decided that he should aim
at the very highest branch of the legal profession—that of
advocate, the Scottish equivalent of a barrister. Soon
Walter was mixing freely with the Edinburgh élite and the
social circle dominated by the younger advocates and the
officers of the garrison. There followed another period of
university study, which began with his attendance at the
class of Civil Law, and he took other classes between 1788
and 1792, including Moral Philosophy from Dugald
Stewart. The good sense and refined sentiment which
were Stewart's supreme values mingled and contrasted
with Scott's other reading, and the two strands were
present together in his mind all the days of his life.

He early attended a class in German, which led directly
to his first literary attempts—translations of ballads, and,
a few years later, of Goethe's *Goetz von Berlichingen*.[7] During
all this period, he read omnivorously in the novel, in
medieval romances, in Ariosto, in Spanish literature. In
1792 he was admitted to the Scottish Bar, and became a
hard-drinking *habitué* of Edinburgh clubs, a participant in
anti-Jacobin riots, and, in 1797, an officer in the local
volunteers. These were the years of Revolutionary war,
and the young quartermaster—who always felt that he

was a soldier *manqué*—compensated for his frustrated longings for a life of action by drilling on Portobello sands.[8] An unknown advocate's life at this time was both leisured and precarious. In order to gain a brief, he had to appear in the Parliament Buildings at nine in the morning and hang about till two in the afternoon, walking the boards, hoping against hope that some Writer to the Signet would ask him to take part in his case. It was a calling that put a premium on verbal fluency, in which men of various ages, all trained in formal rhetoric, whiled away the long hours of waiting in discussion or narration. The more eminent lawyers of Edinburgh had their own particular style, with its own cadences, its own tricks of diction, its own fondness for facetious polysyllabic circumlocution, its own pithiness and pawkiness, its own tendency to make use of all the linguistic resources open to it, including the ability to modulate into the vernacular when the deeds and characters of the lower orders were in question. Above all, it was the style of men to whom time was no object, to whom it was natural to begin a story slowly and deliberately; and then, when once it was fairly under way, to digress into the minute description of attendant circumstances.[9] Walter Scott soon became well known in this society as an interesting *raconteur*, and he was later to carry its style, and even its very tone of voice, into his own prose. That style and that tone of voice were, at one level, emanations and survivals of the Edinburgh of thirty years before, when the towering "lands" of the old town still dominated the city, and all ranks daily intermingled on causeway and in close; at another level, they were the style and tone of Jeffrey's *Edinburgh Review*—judicial, ponderous, and English, moving like a see-saw from one position to the other, but generally ending on a note of finality.[10]

Scott's nature was a highly emotional one beneath the gentlemanly veneer, and perhaps more akin to Burns's than is generally realised. When John Murdoch read *Titus*

Andronicus to William Burnes's family circle, the children
could not bear its mounting atrocities, and nine-year old
Robert burst out that if the play were left in the house he
would burn it.[11] Similarly, when an older cousin of Scott's
had wrung the neck of Walter's pet starling, "I flew at his
throat like a wild cat and was torn from him with no little
difficulty."[12] From this, and one or two other scattered
hints, it is tempting to surmise that the hereditary make-
up of Burns and Scott was surprisingly alike. It is Scott's
misfortune, however, that he succumbed to the spirit of
"catch-the-plack" without much of a struggle. Though he
turned against his father's Calvinism, Scott retained to the
end the habits of diligence fostered by that creed, and
the values of rational control and moral restraint which it
shared with both Augustan ethics and utilitarianism. His
most vivid experiences took place in the world of the
historic imagination, not in personal relations.

We know little of his first love for the daughter of a small
tradesman in Kelso, except that he seems to have dropped
her for snobbish reasons in 1788.[13] His second love for
Williamina Belsches has always been something of a
mystery, and the subject of legend since Lockhart's *Life*.[14]
Williamina, a conventional and rather passive girl from a
higher social position than Scott's own, gave him considerable encouragement, but became engaged to a
banker's son (whom she later married) in October 1796.
Scott certainly believed he had been jilted, and an
interesting comment on the deep passions that
smouldered beneath his self-discipline is provided by one
of his friends in a contemporary letter: "I always dreaded
there was some self-deception on the part of our romantic
friend, and I now shudder at the violence of his most irrit-
able and ungovernable mind."[15] Evidently, it was feared
that he might commit suicide. Once more, we feel ourselves in the presence of a man whose innate temper seems
much more volatile, even volcanic, than anything we
normally associate with the Laird of Abbotsford. His less

immediate reaction was to marry on the rebound—almost within the year—Charlotte Carpenter; and there seems to have been something hysterical, perhaps even factitious, about his feeling for her. Thus his friend Robert Shortreed reported that "Scott was *sair* beside himself about Miss Carpenter;—we toasted her twenty times over—and sat together, he raving about her, until it was one in the morning."[16] Even so, the marriage was soon qualified by the spirit of mercenary common sense, and it began to cool when Scott was able to measure Charlotte against the aristocratic women he met in London. One should put Shortreed's remark beside what Scott himself wrote to Lady Abercorn on 21 Jan. 1810:

> Mrs Scott's match and mine was of our own making and proceeded from the most sincere affection on both sides which has rather increased than diminished during twelve years' marriage. But it was something short of love in all its fervour which I suspect people only feel *once* in their lives. Folks who have been nearly drowned in bathing rarely venturing a second time out of their depth.[17]

The interpretation generally placed on this passage is that Scott believed he had already experienced a much more intense type of love—for Williamina; but Dame Una Pope-Hennessy has argued in favour of Charlotte Carpenter as Scott's one *real* love, maintaining that some of the original events and emotions of the courtship can be deduced from his poem, *The Bridal of Triermain*.[18] Certainly there are passages in the *Journal* which show his distress when Williamina's name was mentioned—over thirty years after the jilting and seventeen years after her death: but his final remark, on 10 Nov. 1827, was: "To me these things are now matter of calm and solemn recollection, never to be forgotten yet scarce to be remembered with pain."[19] The implication is that they *did* cause him considerable pain at the time: a deduction which is borne out by several incidents in the novels, such as his making Jonathan Oldbuck a victim of youthful unrequited love,[20] or his authorial comment on Tressilian's hopeless longing for Amy Robsart:

> Nothing is perhaps more dangerous to the future happiness of men of deep thought and retired habits than the entertaining an early, long, and unfortunate attachment. It frequently sinks so deep into the mind that it becomes their dream by night and their vision by day, mixes itself with every source of interest and enjoyment; and, when blighted and withered by final disappointment, it seems as if the springs of the spirit were dried up along with it.[21]

Some critics, following Adam Scott[22] and Lockhart,[23] have seen in certain of Scott's heroines re-creations of Williamina—Margaret of Branksome in *The Lay of the Last Minstrel*, Greenmantle in *Redgauntlet*, Matilda in *Rokeby*, and Diana Vernon in *Rob Roy*. But these are active, strong-willed, positive creatures who resemble Charlotte much more than the shadowy Williamina, and there seems little evidence for Edwin Muir's suggestion that

> his resolute burial of Williamina probably crippled his imagination on one side and made him incapable of portraying love in his novels. Certain of his women were drawn from Williamina, but they are remote and bloodless versions. It may be that he could not afford to resurrect her, or perhaps the ghost of his father forbade him.[24]

All that can be said is that Scott once loved Williamina; that he once felt pain at her rejection, which his phenomenal memory kept alive for years; that he quite probably also loved Charlotte; and that their marriage cooled off—perhaps also deepened into friendship. But what connexion this really had with his creative life, or with his reluctance or inability to portray sexual passion, must always remain a matter of speculation.

After 1797, Scott's main interests were work and business. His emotional, even vehement nature turned inward to the imaginative re-creation of the past, then outward to the risks and speculations made possible by the embodiment of that re-creation in works of literature sold on a favourable market. In the present century, Scott has sometimes been regarded as primarily an eighteenth-century survival,[25] as a writer who, whatever his innovations, looked backwards to Johnson, Swift, and even Dryden rather than towards such contemporaries as Coleridge and Keats. But this is to underestimate the complexities of literary history. Scott was the culmination of the antiquarian movement of the eighteenth century and the counterpart of his colleagues John Leyden, Joseph Ritson, and C K. Sharpe, yet at the same time he represented the transformation of that movement by a type of imagination that was both "romantic" and historical. Just as Wordsworth's perception of external nature involved not a simple mirror image but a union of subject and object that led to the transcendence of both by "a sense of something far more deeply interfused," so Scott's perception of an antiquarian object—manuscript, broadside, bartisan, or artifact—could in favourable circumstances lead to the bodying forth in fantasy of a past historical environment and social group. And just as the young Blake actually *saw* angels and shepherds, so the young Scott, I am sure, actually *saw* warlike clansmen, feudal lords, and ladies gay, as he wandered in historic places. We have his own admission that he gave himself an active role in these imaginings. "Since I was five years old I cannot remember the time when I had not some ideal part to play for my own solitary amusement," he wrote in his *Journal* for 27 Dec. 1825.[26] In the Introduction to Canto III of *Marmion* Scott answers the question "Why do you write as you do?" by attributing the characteristic cast of his mind to early childhood; his inclination for his own style and subjects is so powerful that he sometimes thinks it innate, and sometimes asks whether it is

> ... fitlier term'd the sway
> Of habit, form'd in early day?
> Howe'er derived, its force confest
> Rules with despotic sway the breast,
> And drags us on by viewless chain,
> While taste and reason plead in vain.

That Scott realised his narrative poems were attempts to re-create and develop further the visual imaginings of a historically minded child is made clear by the continuation:

> And still I thought that shatter'd tower
> The mightest work of human power;
> And marvell'd as the aged hind
> With some strange tale bewitch'd my mind. . . .
> Methought that still, with trump and clang,
> The gateway's broken arches rang;
> Methought grim features, seam'd with scars,
> Glared through the window's rusty bars. . . .
> While stretch'd at length upon the floor,
> Again I fought each combat o'er,
> Pebbles and shells, in order laid,
> The mimic ranks of war display'd;
> And onward still the Scottish Lion bore,
> And still the scatter'd Southron fled before.[27]

Not only the poems, but the Waverley novels themselves, were created by the visual intensity of Scott's historical imagination. That imagination, however, did not feed on emotions and sensations alone. Intellect also played its part—the intellect of that historicism which was one of the greatest achievements of eighteenth-century Scotland, which gave Scott a critical awareness of social history as a process and underlay, one suspects, the paper he read to the Speculative Society in 1791, "On the Origin of the Feudal System." Two other papers he read at the same time reveal an equally intellectual interest in history: "On the Authenticity of Ossian's Poems" and "On the Origins of the Scandinavian Mythology." The type of causation which he favoured—a necessary connexion—is indicated by a summary of the paper on Feudalism which he sent to his uncle, Captain Robert Scott, of Kelso:

> You will see that the intention and attempt of the essay is principally to controvert two propositions laid down by the writers on the subject;—1st., That the system was invented by the Lombards; and, 2dly, that its foundation depended on the king's being acknowledged the sole lord of all the lands in the country, which he afterwards distributed to be held by military tenures. I have endeavoured to assign it a more general origin, and to prove that it proceeds upon principles common to all nations when placed in a certain situation.[28]

At its best, Scott's intellectual historicism—the historiciscm of the Enlightenment—was fused with the "romantic-historical" perception of the past, but the way in which it found expression was determined in part by the state of the literary market. Scott, the dreamer, is an almost clinical example, not of the hero as man of letters, but of the man of letters as hero of industry (the phrase is Benedetto Croce's),[29] enslaved by a system of commodity production which he tried in vain to bend to his will. In satisfying the demands of his public, he provided them with images of virtue and the realisation in fantasy of their more decorous desires. But the value of the novels does not reside in the coincidence of certain private and public wish-fulfilments; it consists in their contribution to knowledge, to the methodology of history.[30] In a hackneyed phrase, "they make the past live"; and whatever lasting artistic significance they possess is connected with their "epistemological" worth.

Scott's first publications (1796), translations of Bürger's "Lenore" and of "Der Wilde Jäger," showed that he was alive to fashionable literary influences, and a meeting with "Monk" Lewis stimulated him to publish a collection of ballads which finally grew into the *Minstrelsy of the Scottish Border*, 2 vols., Kelso, 1802. In 1799 he became Sheriff-depute of Selkirkshire, a post that brought him £300 a year till the end of his life, and in 1806 he obtained the reversion of the office of Clerk of Session, worth £800 a year, but did not receive a salary until 1812. Although these posts involved him in a certain amount of routine work, they gave him security; anything that he might earn by writing would be additional to his salary. In 1802 he began his career as a literary capitalist by lending £500 to enable James Ballantyne, the Kelso printer, to set himself up in Edinburgh, and in 1805 he invested a further £1500 in Ballantyne's business. In 1809, with the establishment of James's brother John as a publisher, Scott became the secret and effective controller of two complementary businesses.

In the intervening years, Scott turned from ballad-editing to romance-editing (*Sir Tristrem*, 1804), the writing of ballad-epics, and miscellaneous literary works, such as his edition of Dryden, with its fine introductory biography. *The Lay of the Last Minstrel* (1805), the first of the ballad-epics, was followed by *Ballads and Lyrical Pieces* (1806) and *Marmion* (1808), the latter being sold to Constable for 1,000 guineas down. His next poem, *The Lady of the Lake* (1810), was even more profitable, for it was published by his own firm, John Ballantyne. Not only did the firm make a handsome profit, but the author himself drew 2,000 guineas directly. For *Rokeby* (1813) he was given £3,000, but it did not sell well, and the Ballantynes were hard hit by their loss. A stronger competitor with a new and irresistible line to sell had appeared on the scene—Lord Byron. After the general market trend had been confirmed by the poor reception given *The Vision of Don Roderick* (1811) and *The Bridal of Triermain* (1813), Scott moved into the field of the prose historical novel with the publication of *Waverley* (1814). There were still three longish poems to come—*The Lord of the Isles* (1815), the journalistic *Field of Waterloo* (1815) and *Harold the Dauntless* (1817): but apart from these, Scott's main endeavours were henceforth in prose—not only the novels, but works like his great edition of Swift (1814), *The Border Antiquities of England and Scotland* (1814–17), the nine volume *Life of Napoleon* (1827), the *Letters on Demonology and Witchcraft* (1830), and his child's history of Scotland and France, *Tales of a Grandfather* (1828–30). Though his plays were unsuccessful [*Halidon Hill* (1822), *Macduff's Cross* (1822), *The Doom of Devorgoil* (1830), and *Auchindrane, or the Ayrshire Tragedy* (1830)][31] his periodical criticism was both sane and acute;[32] the *Lives of the Novelists* (1821–4) and the essays on Chivalry, the Drama, and Romance contributed to the Encyclopaedia Britannica in 1814 and 1822 are still worth reading to-day.

What was the reason for the anonymity of the Waverley Novels? Why did Scott publish some of them as "by the Author of Waverley";[33] others, by an apparently different author, as *Tales of my Landlord*,[34] allegedly communicated by Jedediah Cleishbotham, schoolmaster and parish clerk of Gandercleugh, in the form of manuscripts written up by his assistant dominie Peter Pattieson from material orally supplied by the landlord of the village inn; others still as *Tales from Benedictine Sources*,[35] *Tales of the Crusaders*[36] and *Chronicles of the Canongate*?[37] Scott's motives were certainly mixed: the remnants of a snobbish feeling that novel-writing was not a suitable occupation for a gentleman; an apparent diffidence masking a morbid sensitivity to critcism; appreciation of the value of mystery as a publicity device; a shrewd estimate that if all the novels were unequivocally presented to the public as the work of a single man, they would be immediately dismissed as hurriedly produced pot-boilers; a mischievous love of anonymity for its own sake; and finally, the psychological need for a *persona* and the artistic desirability of a formal frame within which the narrative could be enclosed.

Legends have continued to flourish around the Great Unknown, and it was once suggested by Dame Una Pope-Hennessy that the novels and poems were not written in the order in which they were published, and that some of them were composed many years before they were printed. She claimed that Scott had written the drafts of many novels between 1799 and 1805, citing *Castle Dangerous* (1832), *The Betrothed* (1825), and *The Fair Maid of Perth* (1828) as early works hastily refurbished to meet the financial crisis. *Redgauntlet* (1824) too, in her opinion, "was an early experimental work."[38] So distinguished a Scott scholar as Sir Herbert Grierson found the hypothesis that there existed in 1814 a store of completed manuscripts to draw upon a most attractive one, but pointed out somewhat ironically that "if there was any such reserve to fall back on, it was clearly unknown to his publishers, for they are constantly in a state of waiting for work long overdue." Grierson also notes that, since the manuscript of *Redgauntlet* exists in Scott's handwriting "on paper manufactured by Cowan in 1822," it is unlikely that Dame Una's conjecture about that novel is a valid one.[39] But R. D. Mayo[40] has demonstrated from an examination of the manuscripts and above all of their watermarks that it is extremely unlikely that *any* of the novels were written much earlier than Lockhart and tradition would have us believe, unless we are prepared to hold that in each case Scott copied out the older drafts with his own hand and then carefully destroyed the earlier manuscripts. But Scott's penmanship was so rapid, and his facility at composition so remarkable, as to render this latter possibility quite unnecessary. Unless and until early drafts of these novels come to light in Scott's own hand, it must be assumed that Scott really did work at the phenomenal rate indicated by the dates of publication.

It is easy to make out a case for Scott as potentially the greatest of all our novelists, who failed to be so simply because of his enormous output. The size of that output was dictated by his need for money, which in its turn was determined by his middle-class dream of becoming a landed gentleman—an interpenetration of romance with reality more disastrous than any that occurs in the novels. There were two principal periods of monetary strain. The first took took place in the years around 1813, when the two Ballantynes increasingly became "front men" for Scott's financial manipulations. The profits of James's printing house went to shore up John's business, while John's profits were eaten up by Scott's royalties. The situation was saved by Archibald Constable, whose fortunes were henceforth inextricably involved with Scott's. The publishing firm of Ballantyne was wound up when its stock could be realised; James was confirmed as a printer, but John was transformed into an auctioneer. In 1812 Scott had moved to Abbotsford on the Tweed, and from then on was obsessed with buying more and more land and the over-decoration of his "castle." After the success of *Waverley*, he was able to maximise profits by having one publisher bid against another for his wares,[41] but in the end Constable won. In Grierson's judgment, the prices Scott asked from Constable were "fair and moderate." Nevertheless, "Scott put an undue strain on his publishers by his demands for payment in advance by bills, and on the printing business by the loans which he raised from it for expenditure on land and Abbotsford." Grierson points out that the firm of Constable was itself in a shaky condition during the whole period of Scott's connexion with it, and suggests that if it had not been for Scott and the Waverley Novels Constable would have crashed long before 1826.[42] Lady Scott died in the year of the bankruptcy—the second and worse financial crisis, involving the failure of Constable & Co.—and by Christmas 1827, less than two years after the *débâcle*, Scott had driven his pen to earn almost £40,000. His last years were ones of literary decline—apart from his moving and noble *Journal*—and he died at Abbotsford on 21 Sep. 1832 after his return from a melancholy tour of Italy and Germany, begun at the end of 1831. His creditors were paid off by the posthumous sale of his copyrights.

Most commentators have praised Scott the man even when they condemned Scott the poet and Scott the novelist.[43]

Scott's heroism, however, is not the heroism of a great creative writer, but part of a mask, just as his gentlemanliness, his ease in society, even his love of sport and social entertainment were also part of a disguise. He had little of the artist's dedication to perfection which characterises the literary hero of modern times, and none of the ruthlessness which will sacrifice wife and children, wealth and success to satisfy creative needs. Instead, he became a slave to the business man's neurotic compulsion to work, and to the dreams behind that compulson. Scott's tragedy was that, as a creative artist, he "sold out." His successes, great though they were, were less than they ought to have been, for the simple reason that he would not regard his obligations to literature as having precedence over all other duties. He was a Lost Leader right from the time of the *Lay of the Last Minstrel.* Yet behind the facade of the successful gentleman and honest bankrupt there lay stoicism, melancholy, and resignation; these were the end results of all his innate passion. One is reminded of Ruskin's judgment that Scott's poetry was the saddest that he knew,[44] and of the fact that Scott's own favourite poems were *London* and *The Vanity of Human Wishes.*[45] It is surely wrong to ascribe such abiding despondency solely to memories of Williamina Belsches, and a misreading of history to trace Scott's failures, as Edwin Muir does, to the idea that he "lived in a community which was not a community, and set himself to carry on a tradition which was not a tradition." Muir continues:

His picture of life had no centre, because the environment in which he lived had no centre . . . Scotland did not have enough life of its own to nourish a writer of his scope; it had neither a real community to foster him nor a tradition to direct him . . . If the life he knew had had a real framework, if it had not been melting and dissolving away before him, he would have had a theme worthy of his powers, and he would have had no need to stuff his head with "the most nonsensical trash."

Muir thinks that when, towards the end of his life, Scott wrote "What a life mine has been! half-educated, almost wholly neglected or left to myself," he was expressing "a sense of something lacking in the whole life of his country."[46] But a similar consciousness of neglect and national deficiency did not prevent James Joyce, originally the citizen of a small and backward country oppressed by a powerful neighbour, from writing great fiction. What was there in the Scotland of the early nineteenth century that absolutely prohibited a writer from becoming acutely aware of his country's real deficiencies, as Joyce was later, or from taking up an uncompromising attitude towards his art? It would have been difficult, but not impossible, for a Scottish novelist of 1810–30 to express the fundamental contemporary tensions between Scotland and England; and this, as David Craig has pointed out, would have meant his doing justice "to both the inevitability of a process and the losses involved, while minimising or evading neither."[47] The nearest he came to doing this was not in art but in life—in the public financial crisis of 1826, where he did show himself painfully aware of the losses. In England, as in Scotland, private banks had the right to circulate their own notes. Because so many English banks were in difficulties, it was decided that permission to issue notes should be withdrawn from all private banks in Great Britain. But Scottish banks were not on the verge of collapse; their profits depended on their right to issue notes; and the measure was a blow to the economic prosperity of Scotland, besides being a violation of the Act of Union of 1707. Using as nom-de-plume Malachi Malagrowther, after Sir Mungo Malagrowther, a character in his novel *The Fortunes of Nigel*, he published four polemical attacks on the scheme in the *Edinburgh Weekly Journal*, which contain some of the most vigorous prose he ever wrote. Frustration and disappointment had forced him towards a nationalist position: yet, significantly, his main argument is a class one—the Scots, if their national pride is too sorely affronted, will become turbulent, fractious and even radical, and Scotland be "the most dangerous neighbour to England that she has had since 1639 . . . If you un-scotch us you will find us damned mischievous Englishmen".[48] Let us keep our banking system, and whatever pledges of national identity the union has left us—otherwise the "middling and upper" classes of Scotland may make common cause with the lower orders, and the established system in both England and Scotland be threatened.

Scott's difficulties as an artist were due not so much to any defect of life in the Scottish people—this was an age of industrial expansion and political and social ferment—as to his Toryism, his pathological fear of radical weavers and contemporary mobs, combined with a refusal to put art first, and a disastrous compromise with the market.

REFERENCES

1. V. del Litto, "Balzac et Stendhal," in *Etudes Anglaises*, XXIV (1971), pp. 501–8.

2. Balzac, *Oeuvres Complètes: La Comédie Humaine*, Vol. 1 (1931), Avant-propos, pp. xxviii–xxix.

3. *Scott Bicentenary Essays*, ed. A. Bell, 1973; J. Mitchell, *The Walter Scott Operas*, 1977.

4. See chapter VII, below.

5. Lockhart, I. 1–144.

6. C. F. Fiske, *Epic Suggestion in the Waverley Novels*, 1940, p. xi.

7. Lockhart, I. 144 ff., 229 ff., II. 12, 16.

8. Lockhart, I. 253 ff., 297 ff.

9. H. Cockburn, *Memorials of his Time*, 1909, Intro. and *passim*.

10. *Westminster Review*, I (1824), pp. 206–49.

11. J. Currie, *Works of Robert Burns*, 1800, I. 63.

12. *The Journal of Sir Walter Scott*, ed. W. E. K. Anderson, 1972, p. 590.

13. Johnson, 67–71; *Letters of Sir W. Scott*, ed. H. J. C. Grierson, 1932, I. 1–8.

14. Lockhart, I. 182 ff., 275 ff.; A. Scott, *The Story of Sir Walter Scott's First Love*, 1896, *passim*.

15. Lockhart, I. 278.

16. Lockhart, I. 312.

17. *Letters of Sir W. Scott*, 1932, II. 287.

18. U. Pope-Hennessy, *The Laird of Abbotsford*, 1932, pp. 55 ff., 70–1.

19. *The Journal of Sir Walter Scott*, p. 376.

20. *A.*, p. 13 and *passim*.

21. *K.*, pp. 306–7.

22. A. Scott, *op. cit.*, pp. 15 ff.

23. Lockhart, II. 183.

24. B. Dobrée (ed.), *From Anne to Victoria*, 1937, p. 534.

25. P. Crutwell, in *From Blake to Byron*, ed. B. Ford, 1957, pp. 110–11.

26. *The Journal of Sir W. Scott*, p. 50.

27. *P.W.*, I. 203–5.

28. Lockhart, I. 193.

29. B. Croce, *European Literature in the Nineteenth Century*, 1924, p. 68.

30. G. M. Young, in *Walter Scott Lectures*, ed. W. L. Renwick, 1950, pp. 81–107.

31. Lockhart and Johnson, *passim*.

32. M. Ball, *Sir Walter Scott as a Critic of Literature*, 1907, *passim*.

33. *Guy Mannering* (1815), *A.* (1816), *Rob Roy* (1818), *I.* (1819), *K.*, (1821), *P.* (1822), *The Fortunes of Nigel* (1822), *Peveril of the Peak* (1822), *Quentin Durward* (1823), *St Ronan's Well* (1824), *Redgauntlet* (1824), *W.* (1826), *Anne of Geierstein* (1829).

34. 1st series: *The Black Dwarf, O.M.* (1816). 2nd series: *H.M.* (1818). 3rd series: *The Bride of Lammermoor, A Legend of Montrose* (1819). 4th series: *Count Robert of Paris, Castle Dangerous* (1832).

35. *M., The Abbot* (1820).

36. *The Betrothed, The Talisman* (1825).

37. 1st series: "The Two Drovers," "The Highland Widow," "The Surgeon's Daughter" (1827). 2nd series: *The Fair Maid of Perth* (1828).

38. U. Pope-Hennessy, *Sir Walter Scott*, 1948, pp. 20, 59, 64–9, 99.

39. Grierson, pp. 152, 132.

40. *P.M.L.A.*, LXIII (1948), pp. 935–49.

41. Grierson, pp. 133 ff.

42. Grierson, pp. 147–8, 220 ff.

43. T. S. Eliot, "Byron," in *From Anne to Victoria*, 1937, p. 603.

44. J. Ruskin, *Modern Painters*, III. 291–2.

45. Lockhart, III. 235–6.

46. E. Muir, *Scott and Scotland*, 1936, pp. 12–13, 173, 141–3.

47. Craig, p. 152.

48. *Letters*, 16 March 1826, IX. 471, n.; to Croker, 19 April 1826, 471.

CHAPTER II

THE BALLADIST

Scott's literary development was a progress from ballad collection to ballad imitation; from ballad imitation to the making of ballad epics; and from ballad epics—*via* miscellaneous reviewing and editing—to prose fiction. His ballad collecting began early, perhaps in his sixth year;[1] his ballad imitations were crossed with German influence;[2] and there is this much truth to the Pope-Hennessy theory, namely, that the sources of some of the novels go right back to his antiquarian "raids" into Liddesdale between 1792 and 1798. The information which he then gathered was not necessarily written down, but simply transferred to his retentive memory.[3]

Scott never wrote better, in verse or in prose, than in the *Minstrelsy of the Scottish Border*; and his best verse does not occur in his own professed compositions, "The Eve of St John" and "Glenfinlas," but in the traditional ballads that passed through his hands. Scott's editorial method was sometimes so creative as to resemble a kind of original composition. Just as it is in practice difficult—and even undesirable—to separate Burns's original lyrics from those which he simply amended or altered in the transmission, so with Scott it is often impossible to draw a strict line of demarcation between collecting and composition. Antiquarianism, when developed to a certain level and in a certain direction, becomes itself a form of creation.

The work of recent collectors has demonstrated that a ballad had no real existence apart from oral tradition; when it becomes fixed it is dead, it is no longer a ballad. Earlier commentators like T. F. Henderson[4] were mistaken in adapting the methods and techniques of textual scholarship to orally transmitted work, and in assuming that it is important to discover the "primary text" of a ballad. And they were equally mistaken in forgetting that a ballad is first and foremost a sung composition, and only secondarily a recited poem. Like Bishop Percy before him, Scott was not so much a collector as an editor of ballads, working from manuscripts such as those of David Herd, or versions sent by coadjutors like John Leyden;[5] he was at least two removes from the original sung ballad with its tune.[6] Furthermore, Scott's professed editorial goal was, by blending elements derived from different manuscripts, to produce the "best" text of the ballad concerned. The result was something very unlike the flux of true tradition. At the base of the pyramid were the original ballad singers; then came the writers of the manuscripts, who—when they were themselves cultivated persons —would inevitably be tempted to "improve" their originals in the very act of committing them to paper; and finally the editor, who selected what he thought were the best features of these "improved" versions, ran them together, and often added words, lines, or whole stanzas of his own. If one of Burns's chief merits is that he was an "artist in folk-song," can we deny to Scott the title of "artist in folk-ballad"?

A complicating factor is that Scott, for whatever reason, printed fabricated material sent him by antiquarian friends. He included eleven stanzas in the 1803 version of "The Young Tamlane" ("Tam Lin") which had been sent by Thomas Beattie of Muckledale, though he was clearly aware they were "of a modern cast," and they have no aesthetic merit. Three of the pieces in the complete *Minstrelsy* were concocted by his friend Richard Surtees of Mansforth—"Lord Ewrie," "The Death of Feather-stonhaugh" and "Barthram's Dirge"; and for each of them Surtees provided circumstantial evidence of its

authenticity. Thus the first was written down by "my
obliging friend" from "the recitation of Rose Smith of
Bishop Middleham, a woman aged upwards of ninety-
one, whose husband's father and two brothers were killed
in the affair of 1715."[7] The second "was taken down from
the recitation of a woman eighty years of age, mother of
one of the miners in Alston-Moor, by the agent of the lead-
mines there. . . . She had not, she said, heard it for many
years; but, when she was a girl, it used to be sung at
merry-makings, 'till the roof rung again.' "[8] And the third,
says Scott, "was taken down by Mr Surtees, from the
recitation of Anne Douglas, an old woman, who weeded in
his garden." In order to make the jest more circumstantial, it was communicated in an "imperfect" state, "and
the words within brackets were inserted by my correspon-
dent, to supply such stanzas as the chauntress's memory
left defective."[9] "Lord Ewrie" is an incredibly dull
production, furbished with anachronisms like "I wot"
which are not generally found in ballad diction, but "Bar-
tram's Dirge" is an effective pastiche of the romantic
ballad style.

Though many commentators have sneered at Scott's
naïveté for being taken in by Surtees, there is some
evidence that he was not really deceived, but printed the
ballads out of a sense of obligation to his friend, including
them in the historical section rather than in the class of
imitations in order not to offend him.[10] There is more
positive evidence that Scott was doubtful of "Auld
Maitland," communicated by the shepherd, James Hogg.
Though at first sight this would seem to tell against the
genuineness of "Auld Maitland," it is impossible to deny
that Hogg's mother sang the ballad to Scott in 1802. Since
Hogg recounted the occasion in a poetical address to Sir
Walter printed in 1818 for all the world to see, it is
inconceivable that the scene did not take place more or
less as described. Is it at all likely that an uneducated
woman of seventy-two would learn sixty-five stanzas just

to deceive "the Shirra"? The most plausible interpretation of the facts is that there did exist a genuine Auld
Maitland popular ballad which Hogg's mother recited to
Scott, and that this ballad was the basis of Hogg's
manuscript. Hogg indeed acknowledged that he had
made additions to his manuscript, which were
incorporated by Scott into his *Minstrelsy* version. But the
only alterations due to Scott himself were minor verbal
emendations. No modern scholar of repute believes that
Hogg and Scott between them collaborated to forge "Auld
Maitland,"[11] and the balance of probability is against
forgery by Hogg alone.

"The Battle of Otterbourne" has a theme that goes
back to the sixteenth century, but the *Minstrelsy* version
may owe quite a lot to Hogg. The issue here, however, is
not one of forgery but of the extent to which Hogg altered
traditional material. Hogg sent a manuscript to Scott,
claiming that it was obtained from the "recitation, partly
in prose, of two old persons residing at Ettrick . . . a crazy
old man, and a woman deranged in her mind"; and he
admitted "improving" the verse and turning the prose
into rhyme. "Sure no man," said Hogg, "will think an old
song the worse of being somewhat harmonious."[12]
Whether or not Hogg invented "the two old persons," it
seems incontrovertible that the *Minstrelsy* version owes a
great deal to Hogg, who at this time was not so much a
professional man of letters as a popular poet steeped in the
folk tradition—a literate ballad singer of a kind still found
in Scotland in the early twentieth century.[13] Thus any
emendations he made would be alterations of the same
kind as those spontaneously made by illiterate singers in
the same tradition, and it is significant that the ballad, as
it exists in Hogg's manuscript[14] is a very fine one indeed.
Scott's additional changes are all in the direction of
strengthening the ballad's heroic overtones; they involve
the deletion of an occasional stanza so as to increase the
dramatic concentration, the substitution of more "poetic"

lines from Herd's *Scots Songs*, 1776; and the substitution of
concrete epithets for dull conventional formulas. Scott
selects the best lines from different sources in order to
produce a more concentrated poetry by conflation, and by
cutting out the padding he increases the intensity with
which Percy's death is visualised. These alterations do no
violence to the popular tradition in which Hogg was
working.

   "Jamie Telfer of the Fair Dodhead" tells of an English
raid on Telfer's peel tower, from which the marauders
remove ten cows; of his appeal to a protector, whose
followers manage to rescue the cattle before the
depredators reach their own side of the border; of the
Scottish party's retaliatory raid on the English captain's
house and lands and their capture of a larger number of
cows than the original ten. In the version in the C. K.
Sharpe manuscript,[15] Telfer first appeals to "auld
Buccleuch," the Scott chieftain, who refuses to help him
because Jamie has paid protection money to Martin
Elliot, not to him; Telfer accordingly runs to Elliot, and
the clansmen involved in the subsequent rescue and
retaliation are all Elliots. But in the *Minstrelsy* version the
opposite is the case; Telfer runs first to Gibby Elliot, who
tells him (ST.X) to go to the headquarters of the Clan Scott,
the rescuers here. Andrew Lang attempts to prove from
internal evidence—successfully, as it seems to me—that
Sir Walter must have had before him "a copy of the ballad
. . . not the Elliot version, or the Sharpe copy," which may
well "have represented the Scotts as taking the leading
part"; and he correctly states that, in the absence of
further documentary evidence, "absolute proof that Scott
did, or did not, pervert the ballad, and turn a false Elliot
into a false Scott version, cannot be obtained."[16] And in
the fragment of autobiography he wrote in 1805, Scott
appears to refer to a version of the ballad sung or recited to
him by his grandmother: this, presumably, would favour
the Scotts.[17]

Even if a traditional Scott version *did* exist, it seems fairly certain that Sir Walter altered it more drastically than he altered "Auld Maitland" or "The Battle of Otterbourne." St. XII has the elegiac-heroic note that Scott loved:

> "My hounds may a' rin masterless,
>   My hawks may fly frae tree to tree,
>   My lord may grip my vassal lands,
>   For there again maun I never be!"

It is not so much his own composition, however, as a piece of floating folk-song, found in "Young Beichan" (E.vi), as Child noted;[18] again, "the hawk that flies from tree to tree" occurs in the Kinloch manuscript of "Jamie Douglas."[19] But the description of the skirmish itself is much fuller in the *Minstrelsy* than in the Sharpe version. Three stanzas in Sharpe are expanded into six, and the traditional *motif* of the riderless horse, from St. XII, is repeated to intensify the heroic effect in Scott's STZS. XXXIV and XXXVIII:

> Then till't they gaed, wi' heart and hand;
>   The blows fell thick as bickering hail;
> And mony a horse ran masterless,
>   And mony a comely cheek was pale.' . . .
>
> O mony a horse ran masterless,
>   The splintered lances flew on hie;
> But or they wan to the Kershope ford,
>   The Scotts had gotten the victory.

It is difficult to believe that the expansions in this ballad are not Scott's own work, even although some version of them may well have appeared in his grandmother's account or in other sources now lost. In their finished form they are psychologically motivated by his natural pugnacity, aggravated by the frustrations of lameness. The sentiment thus formed became attached to his own ancestors—imaginatively regarded as almost a collective projection of himself—and generated the spark that set off these heroic stanzas. It is a creative imagination that is at work here, disguised as "editing": an imaginative process nourished by his deepest psychological needs, yet at the same time functioning as the extension of a popular tradition, rather than its negation. And the result is poetry—true poetry at a simple, even an austere level—not the fustian and rhodomontade so often associated with the name of Scott.

"Kinmont Willie" seems a projection of the same ancestor worship apparent in the stanzas added to "Jamie Telfer of the Fair Dodhead," but in its rehandling of traditional material it is more creative—*i.e.*, more analogous to a Burns song—than any of the ballads we have examined so far. Scott surely identified himself with "the bauld Buccleuch"—chieftain of the Scotts—when he hears (STZS. X-XI) that "the keen Lord Scroope" has taken the Kinmont:

> O is my basnet a widow's curch?
>   Or my lance a wand of the willow-tree?
> Or my arm a lady's lilye hand,
>   That an English lord should lightly me?
>
> And have they ta'en him, Kinmont Willie,
>   Against the truce of Border tide?
> And forgotten that the bauld Buccleuch
>   Is keeper here on the Scottish side?

Yet here, as always, it is hard to say what is traditional and what is Scott's own. He calls "Kinmont Willie" one of the ballads he has recovered, and cites the first of the two stanzas just quoted ("O is my basnet?") to prove that it is "very fine indeed," exactly as if he bore no responsibility for its merit.[20] Such mystification is quite consistent with his later denials—before 1827—that he had written the

Waverley Novels. ST. XXXI betrays Scott's hand, in the opinion of both Henderson and Lang:[21]

> "Now sound out trumpets!" quo' Buccleuch;
>   "Let's waken Lord Scroope, right merrilie!"
> Then loud the warden's trumpet blew—
>   "O whae dare meddle wi' me?"

To this we may add that the two final stanzas seem to show Scott or his source creating, in the popular mode, eight lines more concentratedly poetical than anything in the *Lays*:

> All sore astonish'd stood Lord Scroope,
>   He stood as still as rock of stane;
> He scarcely dared to trew his eyes,
>   When thro' the water they had gane.
>
> "He is either himsell a devil frae hell,
>   Or else his mother a witch maun be;
> I wadna have ridden that wan water,
>   For a' the gowd in Christentie."

Scott divided the contents of the *Minstrelsy* into three categories—Historical Ballads (supposed to be founded on actual events), Romantic Ballads, and Imitations of the Ancient Ballad. Those we have been considering fall into the category of the Historical Ballad, as also does "Sir Patrick Spens," into which Scott inserted only minor alterations of rhythm and style. Once more, some of the finest poetry of action in a so-called traditional ballad—in this case, perhaps the best loved of all Scottish ballads—is first printed in the *Minstrelsy*. But the best of the new passages—including the "gurly sea" and "the King's daughter of Noroway"—were supplied by Leyden, who claimed his cousin had them "from a woman in Kelso."[22]

Among the Romantic Ballads, "The Gay Gosshawk" and "The Dowie Dens of Yarrow" have many verbal emendations, and include striking elements from several sources; Scott introduces very little new material, and his poetic personality is evident as an inspired attempt to reconstruct the original. The first printing we have of "The Wife of Usher's Well" is its publication in the *Minstrelsy*, and Child makes the comment: "Nothing that we have is more profoundly affecting."[23] Scott says he got it from "an old woman, residing near Kirkhill, in West Lothian." The MS. has not survived; there is no further reference to her or her ballads in any of Scott's published writings; he had no other version; and he does not say whether he made any alterations. We may suspect that the finest line (in its context)—"Their hats were o' the birk"—is traditional, if only because a similar line ("made o' the bark") occurs in the later version of the Kinloch manuscripts: but who shall say who was responsible—Scott or his source—for the magnificent ST. XI, line 2, "The channerin worm doth chide"? And does not ST. VI sound like a recent addition?

> It neither grew in syke nor ditch,
>   Nor yet in any sheugh;
> But at the gates o' Paradise,
>   That birk grew fair eneugh.

The "Thomas the Rhymer" of the *Minstrelsy* is in three parts, Part II being described as "altered from ancient prophecies" and Part III avowedly presented as "modern, by the editor." Part I, the favourite text of reciters and anthologists, is said by Scott to derive from another mysterious and unidentified lady "residing not far from Ercildoune," corrected and enlarged by a copy from Mrs. Brown of Falkland—Anna Gordon, perhaps the greatest ballad informant of the late eighteenth century. The ballad ultimately goes back to a late medieval romance, a specimen of which Scott printed in his notes. But actually Mrs. Brown's text, from Alexander Fraser Tytler's MS., is the principal source. Child concluded that "it is an entirely popular ballad as to style, and must be of con-

siderable age":[24] but Henderson thought that it was
vamped up from the Romance at "somewhat later date,"
and agreed with Scott that "the tale had been regularly
and sytematically modernised by a poet of the present
day."[25] Scott certainly made his usual creative emendations and additions. In particular, STZS. XVIII–XIX in which
Thomas, in true Scottish style, sarcastically objects to
being "debarred the use of falsehood when he should find
it convenient,"[26] appear steeped in Scott's personality;
they give the ballad a masculine sense of the comic that
lends solidity to the Elfin Queen herself:

> "My tongue is my ain," true Thomas said;
>   "A gudely gift ye wad gie to me!
> I neither dought|to buy nor sell,
>   At fair or tryst where I might be.
>
> "I dought neither speak to prince or peer,
>   Nor ask of grace from fair ladye."
> "Now hold thy peace!" the lady said,
>   For as I say, so must it be."

These stanzas may, of course, be a direct transcript of the
Ercildoune lady's text; but what is certain is that,
whatever their origin, they reflect within a traditional
ballad that amalgam of romance and realism so
characteristic of the Waverley novels.

One of the most beautiful romantic ballads, or rather
narrative lyrics, in the collection is "The Twa Corbies."
In a critical note on the poem, stressing its impersonality
and symbolism—"the hawk, the hound and lady are a
kind of triple symbol of knighthood, of gentry"—T. R.
Henn[27] says it was composed in the fifteenth century.
This, however, is unlikely. Although it certainly embodies
traditional material, as William Montgomerie[28] has
pointed out, the fact remains that it was communicated to
Scott by C. K. Sharpe, who had it from Jean Erskine,
daughter of Lord Alva, "who I think, said that she had

written it down from the recitation of an old woman at
Alva."[29] Comparison with Child's (*b*) version, which was
first printed in Albyn's Anthology in 1818, "from the
singing of Mr Thomas Shortreed, of Jedburgh, as sung
and recited by his mother,"[30] seems to indicate, in Henderson's words, that "the verses have clearly been much
improved either by Sharpe or Scott."[31] Sir Herbert
Grierson converts this into "Sharpe and Scott,"[32] but
more recently M. J. C. Hodgart has claimed that "the
version is largely of Scott's making," and adds that "no
one but an antiquarian purist could object to this reshaping by Scott, since the result is a ballad by any standards
and is good poetry."[33] Whether the ultimate credit for its
reshaping is Scott's or Sharpe's, or Miss Erskine's, the fact
remains that it is one of the loveliest short lyrics of the
Romantic period. "The Twa Corbies" has an underlying
savagery, a heroic quality that is akin to the epic strain in
the ballads celebrating the deeds of the Scott family; its
peculiar excellence arises from a tension between the
romantic overtones of hawk, hound, lady, knight, and
their prosaic opposites ("auld fail dyke,""another mate"),
both coming together in a synthesis which celebrates the
terrible inevitability and impersonality of death, achieved
partly by the repetition of the key adjective "bare".

  The Minstrelsy of the Scottish Border enshrines Scott's place
as one of our three greatest ballad editors, the other two
being Percy and Child. Scott's methods were certainly not
those of the scientific ballad scholar of today, and they
sometimes seem indistinguishable from creation. But that
creativity was a matter of rearrangement and reconstruc-
tion rather than invention—the recombination seen in
Burns's "My luve is like a red, red rose" rather than a
completely new text like "Tam Glen." It is now
recognised that Scott innovated much less than was once
supposed. Of all the hundreds of lines in the traditional
ballads in Scott's *Minstrelsy*, surprisingly few can confi-
dently be said to be his own. Where he did sin was in

running them together in an attempt to come closer to
"the lost perfect form."[34] Towards the end of his life, Scott
himself admitted his error:

> In fact, I think I did wrong myself in endeavouring to
> make the best possible set of an ancient ballad out of
> several copies obtained from different quarters, and
> that, in many respects, if I improved the poetry, I
> spoiled the simplicity of the old song. There is no
> wonder this should be the case when one considers that
> the singers or reciters by whom these ballads were pre-
> served and handed down, must, in general, have had a
> facility, from memory at least, if not from genius (which
> they might often possess), of filling up verses which they
> had forgotten, or altering such as they might think they
> could improve. Passing through this process in different
> parts of the country, the ballads, admitting that they
> had one common poetical original (which is not to be
> inferred merely from the similitude of the story),
> became, in progress of time, totally different produc-
> tions, so far as the tone and spirit of each is concerned.
> In such cases, perhaps, it is as well to keep them
> separate, as giving in their original state a more
> accurate idea of our ancient poetry, which is the point
> most important in such collections.[35]

Yet such wrongdoing made him the purveyor of some of
the finest poems of the Romantic Revival. The ballads
that he edited and pieced together are sometimes
characterised by self-identification with his own freeboot-
ing ancestors; when this occurs, a form of heroic action-
poetry is generated that looks forward to the battle scenes
in the lays and the novels. At other times, they exhibit a
tension between reality and romance that seems fundamental to Scott and made him, much later, at one and the
same time a romantic and an anti-romantic novelist.

REFERENCES

1. Grierson, p. 73.
2. Lockhart, II. 22 ff.
3. W. Montgomerie, "Sir Walter Scott as Ballad Editor," 1956, p. 160.
4. *Minstrelsy*, I. xxvii ff.
5. W. Montgomerie, *Bibliography of the Scottish Ballad Manuscripts 1730–1825*, 1954, pp. xxxii–iii, 21 ff., 94 ff.
6. W. Montgomerie, "Sir Walter Scott as Ballad Editor," 1956, p. 158.
7. *Minstrelsy*, I. 363.
8. *Minstrelsy*, II. 110.
9. *Minstrelsy*, II. 142.
10. Harry, II. 106–114.
11. E. C. Batho, *The Ettrick Shepherd*, Cambridge 1927, pp. 169–82.
12. *Minstrelsy*, I. 283–4.
13. W. Mathieson, MSS.
14. Child, IV. 499–502.
15. Child, V. 249–51.
16. Lang, *op. cit.*, pp. 116–25.
17. Lockhart, I. 18.
18. Child, IV. 5.
19. Lang, *op. cit.*, p. 120.
20. *Letters of Sir W. Scott*, 1932, XII. 173.
21. *Minstrelsy*, II. 57; Lang, *op. cit.*, p 136.
22. M. R. Dobie, "The Development of Scott's 'Minstrelsy,'" 1940, p. 83.
23. Child, II. 238.
24. Child, I. 320.
25. *Minstrelsy*, IV. 92, 97.
26. Child, I. 320, n.
27. T. R. Henn, *The Apple and the Spectroscope*, 1951, pp. 16–18.
28. W. Montgomerie, "The Twa Corbies," 1955.
29. C. F. Sharpe, *Letters*, 1888, I. 136.
30. Child, I. 253–4, nn.
31. *Minstrelsy*, II. 416.
32. Grierson, p. 79.
33. M. J. C. Hodgart, *The Ballads*, 1950, pp. 43–4.
34. M. R. Dobie, *op. cit.*, pp. 86–7.
35. Scott to W. Motherwell, 3 May 1925: Motherwell, *Poetical Works*, 1849, p. xxxiii.

CHAPTER III

THE POET

When the young Scott attempted wholly original poetry in the ballad measure, he at first wrote nothing so good as his interpolations into traditional ballads, few though these were. Years later, in *The Antiquary*,[1] he went back to the method and the mood of the interpolated stanzas of "Kinmont Willie." Using the traditional "Red Harlaw" as his starting point, he gave his own ballad on that topic to one of his impressive spey-wives, Elspeth of Craigburnfoot. Elspeth's ballad succeeds because it is in character, and deliberately fragmentary. The too explicit "Eve of St John" and "Glenfinlas" have been replaced by a mysterious, irrational sequence; and Scott's poetry has gained enormously by his adoption of a *persona*.

Elspeth's ballad is one of a remarkable series of varied lyrics scattered through the novels and longer poems, which are at one and the same time the apotheosis of *pastiche* and the concentrated expression of Scott's own personality. Comparing Scott's lyrics with Burns's, Grierson claims that Scott is more impersonal than Burns: "Even Burns in his recast of folk-songs frequently charges them with more of his personal feelings. . . . Scott's revivals of older strains, aristocratic as often as folk-song, are in a purer style."[2] But Grierson ignores the fact that Burns's best lyrics are often dramatic lyrics, implying a *persona* ("My luve she's but a lassie yet," "Tam Glen," "Thou hast left me ever, Jamie"), while Scott's are impregnated with the spirit of the works in which they appear, which in its turn is Scott's own. Take Lucy Ashton's song from Ch. III of *The Bride of Lammermoor*:

> Look not thou on beauty's charming,
> Sit thou still when kings are arming,
> Taste not when the wine-cup glistens,
> Speak not when the people listens,
>
> Stop thine ear against the singer,
> From the red gold keep thy finger,
> Vacant heart, and hand, and eye,
> Easy live and quiet die.[3]

In its context it is related to the defect in Lucy's character that is part cause of the novel's catastrophe, and is thus the emanation of Lucy, not Scott. At the same time it is connected with preoccupations of the author's own, with the wistful contemplation of temptations. Beauty charmed Scott only in a "respectable" and gentlemanly manner, not in Burns's or Byron's fashion: he would have dearly liked to be a soldier, but his lameness prevented him from serving fully when the kings of Europe were arming. In days when the people required leadership, all he could give them—magnificent though it was—was a picture of their past; the red gold and the wine cup attracted him greatly; often it must have seemed to him that there was an emptiness at the centre of his being—"vacant heart," if not hand or eye; and Abbotsford, for all the bustle of its social life, for all the hunting and fishing and entertaining, was surely in essence a retreat: the direct opposite of political and military life, and a substitute for strenuous action in the real world. Thus I do not think it is fanciful to trace the elements of this beautiful dramatic lyric to Scott's own experience, and to suggest that its mainspring is the author's ironical self-criticism.

Unlike Burns, Scott did not generally have a tune in mind when writing a lyric—but, despite the assertion that he had no ear for music, he could sometimes almost rival Burns in this strain, as in "Bonny Dundee"[4] and "Donald Caird";[5] and his handling of vernacular Scots in this last song has all the vitality of the Scots dialogue in the novels. The most characteristic moods in Scott's lyrics are robust action, elegiac sadness, extreme, even stark poignancy, and the monolithic sublime. For robust action we need go no further than Flora MacIvor's song, "There is mist on the mountain" from Ch. XXII of *Waverley*;[6] for stark poignancy, Madge Wildfire's "Proud Maisie" in Ch. XL of *The Heart of Midlothian*;[7] for elegiac sadness united to a magical strain of high poetry, "Rosabelle" in *The Lay of the Last Minstrel*, Canto VI;[8] and for the monolithic sublime, Rebecca's hymn in Ch. XXXIX of *Ivanhoe*,[9] which contains within itself all the grandeur of the Hebrew strain in Scottish Presbyterianism. There are literally scores of fine stanzas and lines scattered throughout Scott's numerous lyrics, and a handful of songs as perfect as any ever written in Scotland: "Where shall the lover rest?" in *Marmion*, Canto III;[10] the Coronach "He is gone on the mountain" in *The Lady of the Lake*, Canto III;[11] "It was an English ladye bright" in *The Lay of the Last Minstrel*, Canto VI, with its haunting refrain "For love will still be lord of all,";[12] David Gellatley's song in Ch. XIV of *Waverley*, "Young men will love thee more fair and more fast";[13] the song in Ch. X of *The Antiquary* on the inevitability of decay, "Why sit'st thou by that ruin'd hall";[14] the funeral hymn in Ch. XLII of *Ivanhoe*, "Dust unto Dust";[15] and the translation of "Dies Irae" that ends *The Lay of the Last Minstrel*.[16] One can only marvel that the popular handbooks on English romantic poetry and the "romantic imagination" ignore such poems; often, there is not even a single entry for Scott in the index.[17]

Scott's longer poems grew out of his ballad imitations; thus, *The Lay of the Last Minstrel* was originally conceived as a ballad but grew into a longer work under the influence of medieval English romances.[18] He began it in the *Christabel* measure, but soon varied it either with straight octosyllabics, his favourite form, or with one derived from late medieval romances. This latter occurs much oftener in *Marmion*, where octosyllabic couplets are repeated two, three, or even more times, then interrupted by a six-syllabled line, followed by another group of eights, then a second six, rhyming with the first. The effect of the three-stressed line has been well compared to the breaking and falling of a wave.[19]

By the time he wrote *The Lady of the Lake* and the later poems, Scott's lines of eight had developed a "massed and cumulative force" of their own, just like that of the old pentameter;[20] as the line pattern became less broken, his poems exhibited a facile monotony that had been inherent in them from the beginning.

If Scott's versification builds up to parallel climaxes, so, too, does his syntax—a characteristic which Donald Davie has described, in a phrase borrowed from the linguist Roman Jakobson, as "the poetry of grammar." Scott's poetical rhetoric repeats identical constructions in order to produce syntactic augmentation, a "principle of organization" which he uses along with the other repetitive orderings of rhyme and metre. As Davie says:

it is when the traditional principles of order are reinforced by grammatical patterning and parallels that we recognize a poetry thoroughly achieved, structured through and through; and elegant variation, the saying of one thing many ways, brings with it for Scott this additional source of order.[21]

But the "many ways" change what is being said, and give us a poetry that is quite alien to modern English modes, where the short or medium-length lyric is the norm, concentration a virtue, and expansiveness a positive defect. The type of order which is created by all Scott's metrical and syntactic accumulation, by all the elegant variations, may perhaps be regarded as his personal adaptation of that "Celtic ornamentation of a surface" which has often been considered[22] one of the abiding features of Scottish literature. And it exists alongside another principle of order—that of narrative structure, of the tale itself.

In *Marmion* and the later poems, we react in the first place as we do to any other narrative—to the total shape, which in its turn is concerned with the creation and resolution of suspense, with the spectacle of persons and things, with recognitions and reversals, with the contrast and interplay of the expected and the unexpected. Scott's ballad epics consist primarily of situations: rhythms, rhymes, images and "the poetry of grammar" are therefore means to an end. And, as so often in the Waverley novels also, the most striking elements within these situations are description and dialogue. Any of the longer poems provides a typical example; the situations are both visually and dramatically conceived, just as in the most successful modern popular modes—the film, the TV play, and the comic strip—and, what is more important, just as in the best popular ballads in the *Minstrelsy*. Thus the union of sight and sound, of drama and picture, is part of the ballad's contribution to the *Lays*, as it is later part of the ballad's contribution to the novels. Not only are dialogue and narrative linked so that the one interpenetrates the other, as in the scene of Marmion's death,[23] but both dialogue and description are often subordinated to the characters and indeed to their social typology.[24]

Scott's situations are so intensely seen and heard that it seems almost certain they must have existed in the first instance as mental pictures and speech heard with the mind's ear. The creative process with Scott would thus seem to have comprised, firstly, the visualisation of a series of scenes, then secondly, their *translation* into his chosen medium of verse or prose. In the *Lays*, the subsidiary units of the medium itself were often not so much words and images that Scott had impregnated with his own personality after the fashion of a modern lyric poet, as standard currency, like Homeric diction or the stock phrases of ballads and popular poetry. His expressions are often lifted bodily from other poets, or from the *clichés* of everyday life:

> But Isabel, who long had seen
> Her pallid cheek and pensive mien,
> And well herself the cause might know,
> Though innocent, of Edith's woe,
> Joy'd, generous, that revolving time
> Gave means to expiate the crime.[25]

Scott's originality consists partly in his disposition of the larger situations rather than in his language as such. Nevertheless when he is working at full stretch, his "translations" can be intensely and beautifully vivid, as in Canto II of *Marmion*, where two abbesses and a blind and aged abbot sit in judgment on the guilty nun, Constance Beverley, in surroundings of Gothic gloom and horror,[26] or—in *The Lay of the Last Minstrel*—William of Deloraine's wild ride from Branksome to Melrose.[27]

Early critics of Scott's poetry spoke much of his descriptive powers, and one of the most acute of these, Adolphus, pointed out that his descriptions were often conceived in terms of a framed and painted picture rather than as direct renderings of reality. Adolphus also noted Scott's "marked attention . . . to what is called in painting Chiaroscuro"; there are, he said very few of his "poetical descriptions . . . which do not owe part of their beauty to the distribution of light and shade," and he is always concerned "to point out some remarkable appearance of illumination or obscurity."[28] To this might be added his fondness for moving pictures or pageants, especially processions, and his addiction to the poetical equivalent of "glorious technicolor," like the description of Lord Ronald's fleet at the beginning of *The Lord of the Isles*.[29] The pageantry and cinematic quality reach their highest expression in the battle scenes at the end of *Marmion* and

The Lord of the Isles.[30] In *The Lord of the Isles*, Bruce slays a murderer with a brand snatched from the fire:

> The spatter'd brain and bubbling blood
> Hiss'd on the half-extinguish'd wood,
>   The miscreant gasp'd and fell![31]

After Bruce's fight to liberate his ancestral castle from the English,

> . . . on the board his sword he toss'd,
> Yet steaming hot; with Southern gore
> From hilt to point 'twas crimson'd o'er.[32]

In passages like these, or in the incident at Bannockburn where the Lord of Colonsay manages to slay d'Argentine, the knight who has given him his own death-wound,[33] Scott's intensely visual and literal imagination was able to fashion out of his almost juvenile fascination with the horrors of war an anti-poetry of action that is far superior to the more conventional heroics for which he is famous.

In discussing Scott's descriptive verse, Adolphus notes that he never separates nature from human society, and that

> There is, indeed, throughout the poetry of this author, even when he leads us to the remotest wildernesses, and the most desolate monuments of antiquity, a constant reference to the feelings of man in his social condition; others, as they draw closer to inanimate things, recede from human kind; to this writer even rocks and deserts bear record of active and impassioned life, nay sometimes appear themselves inspired with its sensations; the old forgotten chieftain groans in the lonely cavern, and with "tears of rage impels the rill"; the maid's pale ghost "from rose and hawthorn shakes the tear," and the "phantom knight" shrieks along the field of his battles.[34]

Such an attitude to nature is not so much "Augustan" as

"pre-Romantic," for the persons whom Scott finds
inseparable from his lonely places—the chieftain, the
maid of balladry, and the phantom knight—are not those
that would most readily occur to Pope or Johnson. There
is, however, one aspect of Scott's treatment of landscape
which is undoubtedly new—the poetical fusion of landscape with the sentiment of nationality. In previous
Scottish poetry there is much evocation of a
characteristically northern landscape, but without the
specific and obvious infusion of national as distinct from
local feeling. One thinks of the introductions to the various
books of Gavin Douglas's 'Aeneid, of Thomson's *Winter*,
of Burns's occasional sketches of the Ayrshire pastoral
landscape. But it was reserved for Scott to strike such a
note as the depiction of James V's incursion into the
Trossachs in Canto I of *The Lady of the Lake*,[35] or of Loch
Coriskin and the Coolins in *The Lord of the Isles*,[36] or of the
border and lowland scenery of past and present in *The Lay
of the Last Minstrel* and *Marmion*. The union of nationality
with the perception of landscape becomes embarrassingly
explicit in the rhetorical apostrophe which follows the
often quoted:

> Breathes there the man, with soul so dead,
> Who never to himself hath said,
> This is my own, my native land!

The succeeding stanza begins:

> O Caledonia! stern and wild,
> Meet nurse for a poetic child!
> Land of brown heath and shaggy wood,
> Land of the mountain and the flood,
> Land of my sires! what mortal hand
> Can e'er untie the filial band,
> That knits me to thy rugged strand![37]

These hackneyed and oratorical lines exhibit a response to
landscape that seems typically Scott's and which he

renders with greater subtlety in many other passages—as, for example, this one, also from *The Lay of the Last Minstrel*—

> From the sound of Teviot's tide,
> Chafing with the mountain's side,
> From the groan of the wind-swung oak,
> From the sullen echo of the rock,
> From the voice of the coming storm,
>   The Ladye knew it well!
> It was the Spirit of the Flood that spoke,
>   And he call'd on the Spirit of the Fell.[38]

As far back as 1810, Jeffrey seized on his popularity as the most important single fact about Scott:

> Writing for a world at large, he has wisely abstained from attempting to raise any passion to a height to which worldly people could not be transported; and contented himself with giving his reader the chance of feeling as a brave, kind, and affectionate gentleman must often feel in the ordinary course of his existence.[39]

Nevertheless, there are certain limitations in Jeffrey's formulation: for example, the implication that Scott's *personae* always feel and behave like contemporary members of the upper middle classes. This is only partly true, for it overlooks the element of historical empathy: Marmion is a morally mixed character, largely bad but with a suppressed good side, and although Scott means us to condemn him, events and scenes are yet partly seen through his eyes. In *The Lady of the Lake* Roderick Dhu obeys an idealistic clan morality and a fantastic code of chivalry which few "gentlemen" would have followed in the service of the East India Company or the Peninsular War, and the Bruce of *The Lord of the Isles* is an attempt at rendering a leader of Bruce's time and place, not just a nineteenth-century gentleman dressed up in a suit of armour. And there are other effects of which Jeffrey, like many subsequent critics, was not aware, at any rate at the conscious level.

In *The Lay of the Last Minstrel* there is a complex interplay of colours, shapes and—most interestingly—of times. The main structural principle, operating at both the narrative and non-narrative levels, is that of contrast. It is there in the principal surface theme, the conflict between pride and love, which is resolved at the end of the poem when pride is quelled and love is free. And it is there in what J. H. Alexander has seen as the deep underlying theme, "man's attempts to avoid death, his encounter with death, and his learning how to live in the face of death."[40] Alexander explores in detail the poem's contrasts of character, of rapid motion v. slowness, of a vertical scale (tall Branksome associated with pride, Melrose abbey towering high above the bones of the dead) over against a horizontal one reaching out from Branksome to the various regions of the Borders and then beyond Scotland—to Europe rather than to England. There are contrasting sounds, all with thematic or atmospheric value: festal sounds, war sounds, bloodhounds, running water, bird song, the eerie thunderings associated with the wizard Michael Scot, the Last Trump itself. There are contrasting colours, which are not there merely for their picturesque effect—black, white and grey (linked to the death theme); the healthy red proper to love set against the blood red of war and the daemonic redness of pride; the red cross of England and of crusading knighthood. There are contrasting lights and fires—comforting natural fires v. the blazing war beacons, the stars (associated with love), the fire of the final conflagration which will engulf the whole world, the blaze of light from the grave of Michael Scot, the ultimate *lux perpetua* of eternity.[41] And the armour of steel and barred helmets, the stones of Branksome, the abbey and its gravestones, are powerful and repeated symbols of that repression which at the level of character is embodied in

the Ladye. Finally, there is the contrast and interpenetration of *times*. The six cantos are parallel to the three nights
and three days of the main action, with the nights taking
up less space and the days more as the poem advances.
There is a truly extraordinary interweaving of historical
periods and the "manners" appropriate to each—the
early nineteenth century of the author and his readers, the
reign of William III, the mid-sixteenth century when the
main action takes place, frequent evocations of an earlier
middle ages, and finally, the Last Judgment of the *Dies
Irae* in which all times are annihilated and subsumed.

John Pikoulis has recently analysed *Marmion* with equal
sophistication and with equally interesting results.[42] The
underlying theme is concerned with matters as perennial
as *The Lay*'s: the antitheses of time, change and rebirth,
and these are linked to guilt, war and the question of
national identity. As in *The Lay* the nineteenth century is
present—most insistently, through the introductions to
the six cantos, each taking the form of a delightful epistle
to one of Scott's friends, and displaying the author himself
at his task of writing the poem. Scott is thus as central a
figure in the work as Marmion, and the whole is an
artefact through which Scott's inmost feelings are
mediated, much as an image or a symbol might mediate
another poet's feelings." All these emotions—the feelings
of the introductory epistles, the sentiments of the
characters, are swallowed up in "issues of national destiny
. . . great heavings of compulsive feeling which accompany
a nation's travail . . . a larger than human conflict
dwarfing the players."[43] Thus even before *Waverley* had
been completed Scott attempted a new kind of epic—a
kind which achieved satisfactory expression only much
later, with Tolstoy's *War and Peace*.

Scott's ballad epics were both a development and a
negation of his earlier additions to ballads and of his
specific ballad imitations. In form, the ballad epic takes
from the ballad proper its narrative technique of near-

montage, its sudden shifts of place and time,[44] its trick of compressing the events of weeks and years into a single stanza preceded, perhaps, by many lines describing a brief but important dramatic incident.[45] It also adopts the device of building by incremental repetition, as in folk-song[46]—and this, of course, is merely a lexical and stylistic parallel to Davie's "poetry of grammar"; furthermore, it occasionally apes the ballad's compression of dialogue into almost antiphonal ripostes.[47] In content, the ballad-epic experiments with conventions of popular literature that are far more plebeian than anything one might expect to appeal to the "brave, kind and affectionate gentleman" of Jeffrey's critique. "Young Lochinvar" is sung in *Marmion* by James IV's paramour, Lady Heron; con-sidered in the dramatic situation of the whole poem, it is a wily attempt to beguile the king; considered in itself, it is a romantic ballad rendered heroic and masculine by Scott's style and measure.[48] In *The Lady of the Lake*, the poor mad-woman who warns "Fitzjames" of a possible ambush sings of the age-old theme of the "trappan'd" maid:

> For O my sweet William was forester true,
>   He stole poor Blanche's heart away!
> His coat it was all of the greenwood hue,
>   And so blithely he trill'd the Lowland lay![49]

The street singer's cadences are clearly audible behind these stanzas. Again, "Fitzjames's" horn-signal to the royal squires owes more to the Robin Hood legend than to the Song of Roland—the Scottish squires are even clad in "Lincoln green,"[50] and the fine Bacchanalian song sung by a soldier in the same Lay introduces associations drawn from yet another class of popular lyric, the Restoration-type drinking song that swaggers so manfully in d'Urfey's *Pills to Purge Melancholy*:

> Our vicar he calls it damnation to sip
> The ripe ruddy dew of a woman's dear lip,

Says, that Beelzebub lurks in her kerchief so sly,
And Apollyon shoots darts from her merry black eye;
Yet whoop, Jack! kiss Gillian the quicker,
Till she bloom like a rose, and a fig for the vicar![51]

The main situation of the *Lady of the Lake*, that of the disguised monarch wandering among his people, is a favourite one of broadside balladry, and the happily-ever-after ending with the bestowal of "fetters and warden" on the rebel Graeme—the golden chain of matrimony and a virtuous wife—is quite in keeping with the traditions of popular art. The scene in the robbers' cave in *Rokeby*[52] again draws something from the Robin Hood legend, as well as from Burns's *The Jolly Beggars*, while the *motif* of the disguised woman who serves as a page in the wars, used in *The Lord of the Isles*,[53] belongs to the folk just as much as to the world of aristocratic romance. Much of the technique, content, and texture of Scott's ballad epics, then, is creatively developed from the themes, devices, and even *clichés* of popular literature; they represent the successes of *The Ministrelsy of the Scottish Border* raised to a higher level; and, as critics like Pikoulis and Alexander have demonstrated, all these are dovetailed into structures with serious themes and an unexpectedly complex technique.

That strain of melancholy so noticeable in Scott's own ballad imitations is developed in the *Lays* to the point where it becomes mourning for Scotland's vanished independence. When the "last minstrel" is asked by the company at Branksome:

Why he, who touch'd the harp so well,
Should thus, with ill-rewarded toil,
Wander a poor and thankless soil,
When the more generous Southern Land
Would well requite his skilful hand,[54]

his reply is the "Breathes there the man, with soul so

dead" passage already quoted, which soon, however, modulates into the nostalgic

> Still, as I view each well-known scene,
> Think what is now, and what hath been,
> Seems as, to me, of all bereft,
> Sole friends thy woods and streams were left;
> And thus I love them better still,
> Even in extremity of ill.[55]

Thus the romantic-nationalistic attitude to landscape is to some extent a compensation for the desolate state of Scotland in the present. A similar mood occurs in *Marmion*, when a Highland tune puts Scott in mind of Scottish emigrants to Canada and America, chanting

> the lament of men
> Who languish'd for their native glen . . .
> Where heart-sick exiles, in the strain,
> Recall'd fair Scotland's hills again![56]

This is as close as Scott ever comes to what David Craig calls doing justice "to both the inevitability" of contemporary developments "and the losses involved";[57] the trouble is that he does not come close enough, and that his awareness is projected back into the past.

In the introduction to Canto V of *Marmion*, Scott shows himself quite conscious of his escapist role. After a glance at the danger to Kingship from the democratic and anti-royalist movements of his time, he goes on:

> Truce to these thoughts!—for, as they rise,
> How gladly I avert mine eyes,
> Bodings, or true or false, to change,
> For Fiction's fair romantic range,
> Or for Tradition's dubious light,
> That hovers 'twixt the day and night:
> Dazzling alternately and dim,
> Her wavering lamp I'd rather trim,

> Knights, squires and lovely dames to see,
> Creation of my fantasy. . . .[58]

But what he finally beholds in "Fiction's fair romantic range" is the national disaster of Flodden, and in the Spenserians which preface *The Lord of the Isles* he sees himself as

> a lonely gleaner I,
> Through fields time-wasted, on sad inquest bound,
> Where happier bards of yore have richer harvest
> found.[59]

Scott's conscious motive, in these Scottish Lays, seems identical with his intention in *The Minstrelsy of the Scottish Border*:

> By such efforts, feeble as they are, I may contribute somewhat to the history of my native country; the peculiar features of whose manners and character are daily melting and dissolving into those of her sister and ally. And, trivial as may appear such an offering, to the manes of a kingdom, once proud and independent, I hang it upon her altar with a mixture of feelings, which I shall not attempt to describe.

After this, Scott quotes some lines from an anonymous poem, *Albania*, published in 1742, which end:

> Hail! dearest half of Albion, sea-wall'd!
> Hail! state unconquer'd by the fire of war,
> Red war, that twenty ages round thee blaz'd!
> To thee, for whom my purest raptures flow,
> Kneeling with filial homage, I devote
> My life, my strength, my first and latest song.[60]

In the General Preface to the Waverley Novels, however, he tells us that the purpose of his own "latest song"—the prose romances—was to serve Scotland by interpreting her to the English. In this he was following Maria Edgeworth, who

> may be truly said to have done more towards completing the Union than perhaps all the legislative enactments by which it has been followed up.

> Without being so presumptuous as to hope to emulate the rich humour, pathetic tenderness, and admirable tact which pervade the works of my accomplished friend, I felt that something might be attempted for my own country, of the same kind with that which Miss Edgeworth so fortunately achieved for Ireland—something which might introduce her natives to those of the sister kingdom in a more favourable light than they had been placed hitherto, and tend to procure sympathy for their virtues and indulgence for their foibles.[61]

Comparison of these extracts suggests a certain deterioration in Scott's attitude to his native country between the *Mintrelsy* and the Waverley Novels: the pessimistic antiquarian had turned into a loyal subject displaying his ancestors and their quaint dependants to the Conqueror. "Khokol, dance the Gopak."[62]

REFERENCES

1. *A.*, pp. 359–63.
2. W. L. Renwick, *op. cit.*, p. 16.
3. *The Bride of Lammermoor*, p. 26.
4. *P.W.*, I. 5.
5. *Poems and Plays*, 1905, I. 84.
6. *Wav.*, p. 140.
7. *H.M.*, p. 419.
8. *P.W.*, I. 144.
9. *I.*, p. 378.
10. *P.W.*, I. 210.
11. *P.W.*, II. 439.
12. *P.W.*, I. 139.
13. *Wav.*, p. 80.
14. *A.*, p. 89.
15. *I.*, p. 419.
16. *P.W.*, I. 149.
17. M. Bowra, *The Romantic Imagination*, 1961, p. 305.
18. Lockhart, II. 180 ff.; Grierson, p. 80.
19. O. Elton, *Survey of English Literature 1780–1830*, 1912, I. 311.

20. J. Miles, *Eras and Modes in English Poetry*, 1957, p. 118.

21. D. Davie, "The Poetry of Sir Walter Scott," 1961, p. 64.

22. K. Wittig, *The Scottish Tradition in Literature*, 1958, p. 5.

23. *P.W.*, I. 307–12.

24. *L.L.M.*, in *P.W.*, I. 103–4.

25. *The Lord of the Isles*, in *P.W.*, II. 755.

26. *P.W.*, I. 192–5.

27. *P.W.*, I. 73–6.

28. J. L. Adolphus, *Letters to Richard Heber*, 1821, pp. 156–7.

29. *P.W.*, II. 662.

30. *P.W.*, I. 307–8.

31. *P.W.*, II. 705.

32. *P.W.*, II. 749.

33. *P.W.*, II. 771–2.

34. Adolphus, *op. cit.*, pp. 136–7; *L.L.M.*, in *P.W.*, I. 119.

35. *P.W.*, II. 387 ff.

36. *P.W.*, II. 696–7.

37. *L.L.M.*, in *P.W.*, I. 134.

38. *P.W.*, I. 69.

39. F. Jeffrey, *Contributions to the Edinburgh Review*, 1844, II. 493.

40. J. H. Alexander, *The Lay of the Last Minstrel; three essays*, Salzburg, 1978, p. 50.

41. Alexander, p. 75.

42. J. Pikoulis, "Scott and *Marmion*: the Discovery of identity" in *Modern Language Review*, LXVI, no. 4 (1971), 738–50.

43. Pikoulis, p. 742.

44. *P.W.*, I. 242–4; *P.W.*, II. 583–4.

45. *P.W.*, I. 279; *P.W.*, II. 749–52.

46. *P.W.*, II. 713–16.

47. *P.W.*, I. 105–7.

48. *P.W.*, I. 261.

49. *P.W.*, II. 466.

50. *P.W.*, II. 483.

51. *P.W.*, II. 498.

52. *P.W.*, II. 568 ff.

53. *P.W.*, II. 718.

54. *P.W.*, I. 133.

55. *P.W.*, I. 134.

56. *P.W.*, I. 210.

57. Craig, p. 152.

58. *P.W.*, I. 251.

59. *P.W.*, II. 654.

60. *Minstrelsy*, I. 175–6.

61. General Preface to *Waverley Novels*, pp. xiii–xiv.

62. Alleged command of Stalin to Khrushchev; "khokol" is a familiar term for a Ukrainian, as "Jock" for a Scot or "Paddy" for an Irishman.

CHAPTER IV

THE NOVELS—INTENTION AND THEMES

Scott's novels fall into three classes according to subject: stories of English history set in the Tudor-Stuart period (*Woodstock*, *Peveril of the Peak*, *Kenilworth*); stories of English and European History set in the Middle Ages (*Tales of the Crusaders*, *Quentin Durward*); and stories of the Scottish past and near present (*Old Mortality*, *St Ronan's Well*). The superiority of the Scottish novels has been accepted by Scott's best critics from his own lifetime to the present day,[1] and remains true even although one medieval novel, *Quentin Durward*, is of great interest for its presentation of French history, while several of the better novels can be placed in more than one of these classes (*The Fortunes of Nigel*, *The Abbot*, *Waverley* itself).

Yet J. T. Hillhouse, commenting on Coleridge's most favourable judgment on Scott, writes:

> Coleridge drives through and beyond the conception of Scott as a great national writer, as a great exponent of national character, in itself splendid praise, and gives the clue to Scott as an artist whose foundations are broader than national, resting on one of the great dramatic contrasts of universal human nature.[2]

This is the contradiction between Right and Left, between loyalists and the opponents of the *status quo*, which Coleridge termed

> the contest between the two great moving principles of social humanity: religious adherence to the past . . . the desire and the admiration of permanence . . . and the

passion for increase of knowledge, for truth as the off-
spring of reason—in short, the mighty instincts of
progression and *free agency*.[3]

When the greater merit of the Scottish novels is placed
beside Coleridge's statement of the general theme of *all*
the novels, and such later variants of it as that put forward
by the Hungarian Marxist, Georg Lukács,[4] we reach the
conclusion that their basis is national and European at
one and the same time. The Scottish group show "universal" conflict in the particular struggles that Scott knew
best, and originate from his attempt to understand and
identify himself with all the opposing forces that came
together to make the Scotland of his own day. In the
English and European novels he tried to extend the
process, generally with indifferent success. But in the
Scottish novels this most unmetaphysical of men actually
did what Hegel, in Germany, was content merely to think.
Scott was concrete where Hegel was abstract, yet both
were part of the same revolution in human thought. In the
Scottish novels we behold the "unity" of Scotland, conceived as a real nation and not as a bloodless Idea. We see
it dividing into cultural opposites like Highland or
Lowland; or religious ones like Catholic or Protestant,
Episcopalian and Presbyterian; or political ones like
Whig and Tory, Jacobite and Hanoverian: and we
become aware of a shared experience, a fundamental
Scottishness that binds together all opponents even as
they slay and persecute one another. We are shown how
the Scottish nation was in part created by and through the
social conflicts he explores.[5]

Such a summing up of the actual achievement of the
Scottish novels by no means corresponds to what Scott
thought he was doing. The nearest we can come to his own
statement of his general intentions is the passage already
quoted where he says that he was partly led to remember
the mislaid manuscript of *Waverley* by a wish to do for

Scotland what Maria Edgeworth had done for Ireland, and that among his qualifications was his familiarity with both the old type of Scotsman and the new, and with men and women of every social class.[6] His more narrowly aesthetic intentions must be deduced from judgments scattered through the Prefaces, the *Lives of the Novelists*, the critical essays, the *Journal*, and his correspondence. For example, though he admired Swift's and Fielding's mastery of structure, he was disposed to give equal place to strongly-drawn and contrasted characters, and to admire also the "grandeur" of his Gothic predecessors as much as the verisimilitude of Defoe.[7] The Sublime in prose fiction was not solely a matter of landscape and description; it could equally well be embodied in character, as in Richardson's Clarissa. The novelist must strive towards a new creation, since "invention is the highest property of genius": but he must be circumspect in his search for novelty, since the result is the manufacture of "monsters" rather than "models" when mediocrities attempt it.[8] Scott elevates grandeur and variety above the power to arouse the reader's sympathy and pity, and he prefers the harmony and blend of diverse elements to such unity of action as exists in the domestic novel.[9] Variety necessarily includes the comic, which does not exist purely for light relief; thus the "broad and ludicrous humour" of Smollett, kindling the reader into "peals of inextinguishable laughter," is by implication just as worthy as "pathetic composition."[10]

Scott's modesty led him, in the famous *Quarterly* review of *Tales of My Landlord* which he wrote in conjunction with Erskine, to stress that he had not succeeded in fulfilling even such generalised ideals as those summarised in the previous paragraph. He speaks of his own "loose and incoherent style of narration," and "the total want of interest which the reader attaches to the character of the hero."[11] If the selection of a passive hero, the man acted upon by circumstances rather than the man who moulds them to his will, is a part of Scott's conscious intention—a necessary spectator to be the reader's "eye" within the novel—that hero's rejection of passion and his attainment of "happiness ever after" as a propertied gentlemanly consumer are projections back into the past of a contemporary *bourgeois* ideal.[12] Scott did not mean us to worry overmuch about the actions and anxieties of his hero, and described his real purpose as the depiction of *manners*—"some descriptions of scenery and manners, to which the reality gave an interest which the powers of the Author might have otherwise failed to attain for them."[13] It follows from this that it is the faithful rendering of details in the material environment that makes it possible for a novel to convey an overwhelming impression of factual truth.[14] Nevertheless, an excess of *minutiae* can become tedious, and Scott complains of Richardson's superfluous description of clothing,[15] a fault for which he himself has sometimes been criticised. What is required is the unerring selection of just the right environmental traits, just those details that are most significant: the observation of "a distance as well as a foreground in narrative, as in natural perspective."[16] Alois Brandl claims that no writer before Scott had emphasised the concrete objects of the environment in precisely this fashion: "we stumble here upon a new kind of creative consciousness,"[17] which is, of course, manifest in the novels themselves rather than in Scott's critical writings. Scott admired lucky hits in others and achieved them himself. The most masterly of his own touches, however, were not concerned with photographic realism but with making imaginative models of real historical processes and their inner conflicts.

Unfortunately, these models are often grossly imperfect because of the conventional and sentimental plots attached to them. Recent "archetypal" criticism has tried to upgrade Scott by finding an exceptional value in the romance structures themselves. But Scott himself intended the romance and the archetypes as the sugar on the pill; it was history he was really interested in. He thought—or pretended to think—that the romance and the novel did not "stand high in the ranks of literature,"[18] and that it was only in so far as they approximated to epic, or, better still, to history, that they became worthy of serious consideration:

> If . . . the features of an age gone by can be recalled in a spirit of delineation at once faithful and striking . . . the composition itself is in every point of view dignified and improved; and the author, leaving the light and frivolous associates with whom a careless observer would be disposed to ally him, takes his seat on the bench of the historians of his time and country.[19]

In a review of Hoffmann's Novels in the *Foreign Quarterly Review*, July 1827, he dropped the mask of modesty to claim that "the historical romance approaches, in some measure, when it is well executed, to the epic in poetry," and in his Preface to Lodge's *Illustrious Personages* he let slip a sentence that seems to epitomise the manners-painting side of his own intentions: "It is impossible for me to conceive a work which ought to be more interesting to the present age than that which exhibits before our eyes our 'fathers as they lived.' "[20] It is easy to condemn Scott for not writing realistic novels about the Scotland of his own day,[21] but he believed that one cannot know even oneself in the present without being fully aware of one's ancestors.[22]

Of the novelist's character-creations, Scott held that the writer must feel his way into the children of his imagination and identify himself completely with them.[23] This is possible because there is such a thing as general human nature, common to persons of all periods of history; and the writer's highest duty is to apply his knowledge of human beings, derived from the observation of his own mental processes and those of others, to characters of an

alien time and situation. Such was Scott's theory. At his
best, however, he rendered the *particulars* of human
behaviour with greater attention to the variations due to
differences of time and place than his creed would seem to
warrant. "There followed for him," says Brandl, "the
further conclusion that all those people who are worth the
trouble of describing in novels always act rightly from
their standpoint, and that we would act in just the same
fashion if we were in their place."[24] When Scott succeeds
in making the past come alive for us, his characters are not
so much persons of the early nineteenth century transpor-
ted into the seventeenth century or the Middle Ages, as
persons of those epochs themselves, tinged with just suf-
ficient anachronism to enable us to understand them; and
when he presents us with Jacobites and Whigs, Cavaliers
and Puritans—all "acting rightly from their standpoint"
—he is not glossing over antagonisms with a
false veneer of tolerance, but showing us what Hegel
called "the spirit opposing itself and overcoming itself as
the really hostile obstacle to its own purpose."[25]

Scott's themes are of two sorts: superficial and conventional themes, inherited from the past, and "inner
themes," proceeding from his deepest intentions and from
the exploratory activity of his composition. In *Woodstock*, a
typical Tudor-Stuart novel, the superficial themes are the
Romeo and Juliet love of young Everard, a moderate
Presbyterian, and Alice, daughter of the old-fashioned
Royalist, Sir Henry Lee; the anti-Puritanism manifest in
the gulling of the Parliamentary Commissioners, sent to
take over Woodstock Palace, by a series of pseudo-
supernatural events manipulated by the hypocritical
secret agent Tomkins in collusion with Royalist plotters;
and conscious Tory principles reflected in incidental
comments which oppose democracy and praise the values
of aristocracy.[26] It is better to group all three strands as
thematic, rather than discuss the first two as com-
positional, and the third under the head of the novelist's

philosophy. The inner themes of *Woodstock* concern such obvious conflicts as Cavalier versus Puritan deployed in contrasting characters like Cromwell and the young Charles II; like Wildrake, the royalist scapegrace created from scraps of Restoration drama; or like the caricatured sectarians and army extremists. Such characterisation, however, is introduced mainly in the interests of that variety and historical concreteness which it was part of Scott's intention to provide. The real "inner theme" is concerned with the relationship between what Hegel termed "maintaining personalities" and "world-historical" personalities.[27] This is brought out in quite an early scene. Everard has tried to protect Sir Henry from the Parliamentary Commissioners who have ousted him from his position as Chief Ranger in the Royal Forest and have their eye on his own estate, but the interview ends in a quarrel. Old Goody Jellicot and Phoebe Mayflower, who acts as Alice's maid, are "maintaining personalities"; they belong to the common people whose daily activities must continue irrespective of the whims of their betters, of the shift of political and social power from one ruling group to another:

Phoebe Mayflower blubbered heartily for company, though she understood but little of what had passed; just, indeed, enough to enable her afterwards to report to some half-dozen particular friends that her old master, Sir Henry, had been perilous angry, and almost fought with young Master Everard, because he had wellnigh carried away her young mistress. 'And what could he have done better,' said Phoebe, 'seeing the old man had nothing left either for Mrs Alice or himself? and as for Mr Mark Everard and our young lady, oh! they had spoken such loving things to each other as are not to be found in the history of Argalus and Parthenia, who, as the story-book tells, were the truest pair of lovers in all Arcadia and Oxfordshire to boot.'[28]

The antiquarian David Laing notes that *The Most Pleasant and Delightful History of Argalus and Parthenia* was a chap-book very popular in the seventeenth century.[29] Its mention has more than documentary value; it is one of those "lucky hits" Scott so admired in others. The chap-book story, though a popularisation of an upper-class tale, now belonged to popular culture; it was as much a part of Phoebe's mental life as folk-song and folk tale; and Scott's glance at it shows his awareness of how such persons' judgment interacts with inherited culture patterns. The passage is shot through with an unobtrusive irony that implies, at a superficial level, Phoebe's inferiority to the author; and, at a deeper level, that Phoebe's reactions are truer than Sir Henry's or Everard's or even Alice's. The scene continues:

> Old Goody Jellicot had popped her scarlet hood into the kitchen more than once while the scene was proceeding; but, as the worthy dame was parcel blind and more than parcel deaf, knowledge was excluded by two principal entrances; and though she comprehended, by a sort of general instinct, that the gentlefolk were at high words, yet why they chose Joceline's hut for the scene of their dispute was as great a mystery as the subject of the quarrel.

Our amusement at the old lady's incomprehension is compounded of a doubtless unworthy smile at the foibles of senility; of the upper-class observer's amused superiority towards the servants; and of the realisation that her mystification reflects the insignificance of the gentry's concerns. From Goody Jellicot's point of view, and Phoebe's, gentlefolk's high words are "bot wind inflat in other mennis eiris";[30] their quarrels mean little compared with the sufferings and "hard darg" of the poor.

Alice is deeply upset by what has happened; and Phoebe, "though too ignorant and too simple to comprehend the extent of her distress," nevertheless gives her

greater help than a confidante of her own class could have
provided by affording her "material assistance, in lack of
mere sympathy." There follows a delightfully imagined
miniature:

> With great readiness and address, the damsel set about
> everything that was requisite for preparing the supper
> and the beds; now screaming into Dame Jellicot's ear,
> now whispering into her mistress's and artfully
> managing as if she was merely the agent under Alice's
> orders.

In case we have missed the meaning of the scene, Scott
underlines it for us in the last sentence of the chapter:

> Alice had less quiet rest in old Goody Jellicot's wicker
> couch, in the inner apartment; while the dame and
> Phoebe slept on a mattrass, stuffed with dry leaves, in
> the same chamber, soundly as those whose daily toil
> gains their daily bread, and whom morning calls up
> only to renew the toils of yesterday.[31]

If the "Romeo and Juliet" theme of Everard's love for
Alice belongs to the surface of the novel in a way that, in
The Bride of Lammermoor, the love of Lucy and Ravenswood
does not, it still has a connexion with the deeper theme of
the relationship between social basis and social super-
structure. The historical conflicts raging in England
between Cavalier and Puritan, Presbyterian and Independent are ephemeral when set beside the values of true love
and social continuity based on the family. Thus Scott
unites yet another of the values of folk and popular poetry
("Love will find out the way") with a statement similar to
Tolstoy's at the end of *War and Peace* when we see Natasha
and Pierre content with the responsibilities and cares of
ordinary family life. Everard is a gentlemanly Everyman,
a moderate Presbyterian emblematic of the continuity of
English history as a " 'middle course' asserting itself
through the struggle of extremes . . . the age-old

steadfastness of English development amidst the most terrible crises."[32] It is this which underlies the final pageantry—Charles II's progress through London on the occasion of his happy Restoration—uniting in a single scene all the historically conceived values of the book.

In the medieval novels, too, we find superficial themes alongside an underlying deeper theme or themes. In *Ivanhoe*, for example, there are so many outer themes that most readers tend to write it off as a sentimental romance for children. But just as *Woodstock* gives us not real history but a historical model of revolution and continuity, so *Ivanhoe* gives us a model, or perhaps even a myth, that bears a significant relationship to a general historical process. *Ivanhoe*, behind the superficial themes and in spite of the anachronisms, presents a paradigm of how new nations are created out of subsidiary tribal or national units; and it is because of his experiences as a Scotsman that Scott was able to understand this general process intuitively. Both Rebecca and Rowena are representatives of oppressed races and nationalities; Cedric's attitude to Ivanhoe reminds one of the behaviour of the older generation of Scots towards their sons and grandsons after the Union of 1707; and the following generalisation made by Cedric surely owes its passion to the imaginative transference of Scottish feelings towards the English, or Highland feelings towards Lowlanders, into Saxon feelings towards Normans:

We made these strangers our bosom friends, our confidential servants; we borrowed their artists and their arts, and despised the honest simplicity and hardihood with which our brave ancestors supported themselves; and we became enervated by Norman arts long ere we fell under Norman arms. Far better was our homely diet, eaten in peace and liberty, than the luxurious dainties, the love of which hath delivered us as bondsmen to the foreign conqueror![33]

In this comment, Cedric glances at a favourite theme of
Scott's, the nature of heroism, here seen Rousseauistically
in contrast to civilisation. It is, however, in the depiction of
Coeur-de-Lion as the bearer of historical destiny—as the
type of the truly national king who can attract the loyalties
of formerly antagonistic sub-groups—that Scott realises
his *model*, the serious concern behind the pageantry and
romance of *Ivanhoe*.

As a whole, the Scottish novels are even more fundamentally concerned with necessity and heroism than
those of the other two classes, and they also show a more
complex blending of superficial and "deep" themes. The
short stories "A Highland Widow"[34] and "The Two
Drovers"[35] are thematic microcosms of much that is most
vital in *Waverley*, *Rob Roy*, *The Bride of Lammermoor*, and
Redgauntlet; they stem from the same preoccupations as
these novels. In "A Highland Widow" the main theme is
the relativity of moral codes and their social determinants
as illustrated by the conflict between old and new in
Highland society after the Forty-Five—between Elspat
McTavish, whose husband had been killed in her
presence by a Hanoverian punitive detachment, and her
grown up son, who, in the new conditions of some fifteen
years later, is driven by her taunts to prove his manhood in
some active way. But the combative life which Hamish
chooses is that of a soldier in one of the new Highland regi-
ments overseas, in the service of the hated Hanoverians;
from Elspat's point of view, this is treachery. When he
comes home to say farewell he tells her that if he does not
report to Fort Augustus in seven days he will be shot as a
deserter. Elspat gives him a potion that puts him to sleep
for the remainder of his furlough, in the hope that when he
finds he has overstayed his leave he will grow into the
outlaw bandit that he would not become by free choice.
Though he is as fiercely devoted to honour as his father
ever was, Hamish interprets the concept in a new way: he
decides not to try to escape punishment.

But whether his intention was to yield himself peaceably into the hands of the party who should come to apprehend him, or whether he purposed, by a show of resistance, to provoke them to kill him on the spot, was a question which he could not himself have answered.

In the heat of the moment, and under the influence of his mother's whispered reminder " 'The scourge—the scourge, my son—beware the scourge,' " he shoots the sergeant in charge, his best friend. When he is executed, he is "more glad to die than ever he was to rest after the longest day's hunting." Elspat turns into a crazed Wordsworthian figure, and she dies with an animal's dignity taught by instinct "to withdraw herself from the sight of her own race, that the death-struggle might take place in some secret den, where, in all probability, her mortal relics would never meet the eyes of mortals."[36]

The themes of old *versus* new, of heroism *versus* commercial civilisation, of the sublimity of Highland honour are perfectly integrated with plot, dialogue, and character in an almost Aristotelian pattern of classical spareness and nobility. Only the explaining away of the supernatural detracts from its beauty, but even this imperfection is less noticeable than in most of Scott's works. "The Two Drovers" has still less of the supernatural about it—only the prophecy of doom which his spey-wife aunt makes to Robin Oig McCombich before he sets out to drive his cattle from the Highlands to Doune Fair in Westmoreland. When he falls out with his Yorkshire friend Harry Wakefield over pasture rights for the night, Harry wishes to settle the matter by fisticuffs, but Robin has no skill at this English accomplishment, and he is knocked out. Refusing the victor's friendship, he goes back for his skene-dhu; returns, and stabs Harry in the heart. Scott never showed his narrative genius to better effect than in this tragedy arising from the conflict

of utterly different ways of life—Hegel's "war of good
against good."[37] The only blemish is the interpolated
explanation in which he leans over backwards to describe
"the generosity of the English audience" at Robin's trial,
who were "inclined to regard his crime as the wayward
aberration of a false idea of honour rather than as flowing
from a heart naturally savage, or perverted by habitual
vice." Scott redeems himself, however, by giving Robin
the last word: "But he replied indignantly to the observations of those who accused him of attacking an unarmed
man. 'I give a life for the life I took,' he said, 'and what can
I do more?' "[38] Robin's integrity makes the same point as
Evan Dhu's rebuke to the "Saxon gentlemen" on a similar
occasion in *Waverley*.[39]

In the Tudor-Stuart and medieval novels the themes of
heroism and necessity tend to be submerged by what is
sometimes termed "tushery"; in the Scottish novels they
are presented in organic relationship to the Scotland of
Scott's own day. "All his great characters," says Lord
David Cecil, "are the children of small communities, close
corporations, remote localities, age-old traditions, the
sharp angles cut by whose influence have been unmodified
by contact with the great changing, impersonal,
cosmopolitan world."[40] This is to see only the particular,
and to ignore the universal which is expressed through the
particular. Commenting on this very aspect of the Scottish
novels, Lukács describes Scott as a master of the historical
imagination who was at his best in dramatising the
passage from gentile society to civilisation, creating an
image of a process equivalent to "what in Morgan, Marx
and Engels was worked out and proved with theoretical
and historical clarity."[41] In *A Legend of Montrose* Scott's
awareness of the inevitability of this transformation is
underlined, in a speech of Allan McAulay, a "seer" who
knows the side he supports is doomed:

"The die is cast for us all, Sir Duncan," replied Allan,

looking gloomy, and arguing on his own hypochondriac feelings: "the iron hand of destiny branded our fate upon our forehead long ere we could form a wish or raise a finger in our own behalf. Were this otherwise, by what means does the seer ascertain the future from those shadowy presages which haunt his waking and his sleeping eye? Nought can be foreseen but that which is certain to happen."[42]

That which is certain to happen comprises, firstly, Montrose's victory, inevitable because the balance of clan forces has tilted against his opponents, the Campbells and their allies; and, secondly, his ultimate defeat, because by the very nature of clan psychology his followers are incapable of carrying the war into England and campaigning against Parliament. They are interested not in national, but in clan politics, and that is Montrose's undoing.

In *Waverley* subsidiary folk and "archetypal" themes, as well as secondary historical themes, such as the relation of ends to means, of political idealism to political expediency, are deployed against the background of the general psychological conflict between illusion and reality. The novel's main concern, however, is still with the necessity of the dissolution of the clans, portrayed as the movement of masses of men in action, and seen through the eyes of a middle-of-the-road hero who returns to the humdrum existence of a landed gentleman with only a few glances back towards his own romantic dreams and the heroism of a vanished social order.[43] Rob Roy, the swashbuckling cateran, admits that a bandit's life is all very well for himself, but that it would be better for his own sons to move with the times and follow another occupation.[44] The mediocre hero of *Rob Roy*, Francis Osbaldistone, rejects both English Jacobite-Toryism and the values of the Clan McGregor; willy-nilly, he is forced to lean on the *bourgeois* philistinism of Bailie Nicol Jarvie, who is both a comic figure and the representative of progress. David Daiches sees as the most important aspect of *Rob Roy* "the necessity of sacrificing heroism to prudence, even though heroism is so much more attractive."[45] In this novel both heroism and necessity are socially conceived, almost as in Engels' analysis of the break-up of tribalism:

> The power of this primitive community had to be broken. . . . But it was broken by influences which from the very start appear as a degradation, a fall from the simple moral greatness of the old gentile society. The basest interests—mean greed, brutal appetites, sordid avarice, selfish robbery of the common wealth— inaugurate the new, civilised, class society. . . .[46]

There is an impassioned moralism here which is part of Rousseau's legacy to Marxism; it goes right back to classical myths of the Golden Age; and it is very close to a strand that runs through Scott's tales of Highlands and Lowlands. Scott's heroes are always brought to realise that utilitarianism and property are necessary;[47] in a Keatsian phrase applied to Scott by Dr Tillyard they always wake up on the cold hill side[48]—and make themselves believe it is warm.

In *Old Mortality* the social conflict is a more developed one between westland Whigs and Government troops employed to force an alien religion upon the stern and independent peasantry. Two kinds of heroism are contrasted—that of the leaders, and that of the "world maintaining personalities," represented by Cuddie Headrigg. Cuddie is a low-life comic character who also has a serious role to play. To the extremists of both sides he seems indifferent, apathetic, and even cowardly, but his prudence represents the values of the social base, and he helps the moderate hero, Henry Morton, just as Phoebe acts for Alice and Everard in *Woodstock*. The terrible but debonair Graham of Claverhouse and the revolutionary fanatic Balfour of Burley embody opposite types of heroism; each is in contradiction to the levelling grayness of historical necessity, each is destroyed by it. John Buchan saw the theme of *Redgauntlet*, set two decades after the Forty-Five, as "the iron compulsion of fate":[49] but, as Daiches has noted, Redgauntlet's heroism is intentionally melodramatic and inflated because he is rowing against the stream of destiny.[50] His rhodomontade is a quality of his chosen role. In *Guy Mannering*, whose action takes place in Scott's own youth, the theme of old-fashioned heroism *versus* modern common-sense utility has almost receded into the background beside the subsidiary mystification engendered by the "lost heir" plot and the attempt to render an English, not a Scottish gentleman. Meg Merrilies and the gipsies take the place of Highland clansmen and Border reivers, as do Wandering Willie in *Redgauntlet*, and Edie Ochiltree and the Mucklebackits in *The Antiquary*. The *dénouement* of *Guy Mannering* is dependent on Councillor Pleydell, one of Scott's most vital and loveable legal eccentrics; and this implies that kindliness, tolerance, and humour—ideal virtues of the eighteenth-century compromise and of a Scottish family lawyer of the old school—are capable of "mediating between extremes and enabling the new world to preserve, in a very different context, something of the high generosity of the old."[51] But in *St Ronan's Well*, his only really contemporary novel, the opposites have indeed flown apart. The older themes have become swamped by humorous characters like Meg Dods, the innkeeper, and Pleydell has turned into Touchwood, a pre-Dickensian, Brownlow-like *deus ex machina*. The opposition between old and new manifests itself in the pathos of declining aristocrats like Clara Mowbray and her brother; in the visual contrast between the traditional world of the Village and the socialite world of the Well; and in the thematic proverb, "new lords, new laws."[52] Like Dickens's Veneerings, Scott's Earl of Etherington prefers the show of things to their substance.

When Tyrrel says he is willing to give up his claim to the earldom for Clara's sake, Captain Jekyl replies:

'To a proposal so singular as yours, I cannot be expected to answer, except thus far—the character of the peerage is, I believe, indelible, and cannot be resigned or assumed at pleasure. If you are really Earl of Etherington, I cannot see how your resigning the right may avail my friend.'

'You sir, it might not avail,' said Tyrrel, gravely, 'because you, perhaps, might scorn to exercise a right or hold a title that was not legally yours. But your friend will have no such compunctious visitings. If he can act the earl to the eye of the world, he has already shown that his honour and conscience will be easily satisfied.'[53]

Real honour and conscience seem to be relics of a former age, and can be furthered only through the artificial exertions of fairy godfathers like Touchwood. Otherwise, there is nothing but the cold hill side.

REFERENCES

1. Hillhouse, *op. cit.*, Ch. III and *passim.*
2. *Op. cit.*, p. 153.
3. S. T. Coleridge, *Biographia Epistolaria*, 1911, II. 181.
4. Lukács, p. 31.
5. *Op. cit.*, pp. 28–9.
6. General Preface to the *Waverley Novels*, pp. xiii–xiv.
7. *M.P.W.*, I. 189, 259, 313 ff.
8. *M.P.W.*, I. 358.
9. *M.P.W.*, I. 275–6.
10. *M.P.W.*, I. 277.
11. *Quarterly Review*, XVI (1817), pp. 431–2.
12. Welsh, *passim.*
13. General Preface, p. xv.
14. *M.P.W.*, I. 189.
15. *M.P.W.*, I. 252.
16. *M.P.W.*, I. 189.
17. A. Brandl, "Walter Scott über sein dichterisches Schaffen," 1925, p. 361.
18. *The Abbot*, p. ix.
19. *Quarterly Review*, XVI (1817), p. 467.
20. Ball, *op. cit.*, p. 132.
21. Craig, pp. 221 ff.
22. Ball, *op. cit.*, p. 133.
23. *M.P.W.*, I. 189.
24. Brandl, *op. cit.*, p. 363.

25. Lukács, p. 28.
26. *W.*, pp. 264–5.
27. Lukács, p. 39.
28. *W.*, pp. 53–4.
29. *W.*, p. 54, n.
30. Henryson, "Testament of Cresseid," l. 463.
31. *W.*, p. 55.
32. Lukács, p. 37.
33. *I.*, p. 191.
34. *Waverley Novels*, XIX. 397–458.
35. *Op. cit.*, XX. 317–47.
36. "The Highland Widow," pp. 443–4, 451, 458.
37. A. C. Bradley, *Oxford Lectures on Poetry*, 1911, p. 86.
38. "The Two Drovers," pp. 347, 343.
39. *Wav.*, p. 421.
40. D. Cecil, "Sir Walter Scott," 1932, p. 279.
41. Lukács, p. 56.
42. *A Legend of Montrose*, p. 228.
43. Welsh, pp. 147–8 and *passim*.
44. *Rob Roy*, pp. 346 ff.
45. D. Daiches, *A Critical History of English Literature*, 1960, II. 845.
46. F. Engels, *Origin of the Family, Private Property, and the State* (1884) tr. A. West and D. Torr, Sydney 1942.
47. Welsh, pp. 114 ff.
48. E. M. W. Tillyard, *The Epic Strain in the English Novel*, 1958, p. 73.
49. Tweedsmuir, *Sir Walter Scott*, 1932, p. 265.
50. Daiches, *op. cit.*, II. 851.
51. *Op. cit.*, II. 839.
52. *St Ronan's Well*, p. 146.
53. *Op. Cit.*, p. 317.

CHAPTER V

THE NOVELS—CHARACTER, METHOD, STYLE

It is said that Scott's characterisation is not analytic,[1] but this is a view that requires qualification. His middle-of-the-road heroes are constantly soliloquising in the manner of characters in Shakespearian drama, and their conscious thoughts—and sometimes their unconscious ones as well—are frequently revealed by direct authorial comment. Scott was theoretically aware of the complexity of human motive, and despite his acknowledgment of the difficulty of the task,[2] he did not forbear to analyse as well as to present. When Waverley ascends the glen to make his proposal to Flora, his mental conflict is disclosed in terms of his own musings, that is, of his own analysis of his conscious feelings;[3] and when he makes up his mind to leave Glennaquoich and appease his military superiors, his decision is accompanied by an inward political debate that involves the analysis of others' actions as well as his own—Rose's "anxiety for his safety," Flora's "self-devotion to the cause . . . united to her scrupulous rectitude as to the means of serving it."[4] Scott is aware that his characters are often unconscious of their real feelings or motives. During Waverley's stay at Tully Veolan, "the sentiments" of Rose Bradwardine are "gradually, and without being conscious, assuming a shade of warmer affection"[5] towards Waverley, who is subconsciously attracted to Rose, even though he believes he is falling in love with Flora.[6] Can such commentary, and such presentation, be called anything other than a form of analysis?

To see Scott's analytical method at its crudest one has only to turn to Ratcliffe's account of the Black Dwarf's psychological development, where everything in Elshie's career from his early benevolence to his later misanthropy is ascribed to his deformity.[7] Scott's psychological scheme is no doubt valid, but his explanation is so incredibly laboured that one can only marvel at its occurrence in the pages of a reputable writer. A more artistic example of the same method occurs when Rowena begs her captor de Bracy to save Ivanhoe: Scott says her disposition is "naturally that which physiognomists consider as proper to fair complexions—mild, timid, and gentle," but because she has had her own way from infancy, she has acquired a "fictitious" haughtiness and habit of command that collapses completely before "a man of a strong, fierce and determined mind, who possessed the advantage over her, and was resolved to use it."[8] Like so many in the early nineteenth century—Balzac, for example, and Elizabeth Gaskell—Scott seems to have believed in physiognomy as an index to character.

Scott is generally held to be a singularly unintellectual writer, but an examination of his method of presenting character shows him applying his intellect—and the psychological theories of his age—to the description of states of mind. He does so even in dialogue, as in the anachronistic passage where Ulrica sees her whole past life as determined by such isolated and abstractly conceived sentiments as "the maddening love of pleasure, mingled with the keen appetite of revenge, the proud consciousness of power—draughts too intoxicating for the human heart to bear, and yet retain the power to prevent.'"[9] Scott's psychological acumen is often aroused by the "sex war." There is an extraordinary scene in *The Abbot* where the page Roland Graeme sees from his inn window a form which he takes to be that of the girl he loves, Catherine Seyton, disguised in youth's attire. It is, however, Catherine's brother Henry, who possesses, like his sister, "the bright and clustered tresses, the laughing full blue eyes, the well-formed eyebrows, the nose with the slightest possible inclination to be aquiline, the ruby lip, of which an arch and half-suppressed smile seemed the habitual expression." This sexually ambiguous figure arouses considerable excitement in Roland when "she" whips a lounger "in a manner which made him spring aside, rubbing the part of the body which had received so unceremonious a hint that it was in the way of his betters." The whole situation is a comic one, and Scott's analytical psychology—in this case, Roland's spur-of-the-moment self-analysis—is part of the comedy:

> While the disguised vestal looked with unabashed brow, and bold and rapid glance of her eye, through the various parties in the large old room, Roland Graeme, who felt an internal awkward sense of bashful confusion, which he deemed altogether unworthy of the bold and dashing character to which he aspired, determined not to be browbeaten and put down by this singular female, but to meet her with a glance of recognition so sly, so penetrating, so expressively humorous, as should show her at once he was in possession of her secret and master of her fate, and should compel her to humble herself towards him, at least into the look and manner of respectful and deprecating observance.
>
> This was extremely well planned; but, just as Roland had called up the burning glance, the suppressed smile, the shrewd, intelligent look which was to ensure his triumph, he encountered the bold, firm and steady gaze of his brother or sister page . . .[10]

Scott has a much shrewder appreciation of the psychology of lovers than he is generally given credit for: but he understands them intellectually rather than emotionally. Even that most wooden of heroines, Julia Mannering, can describe a scuffle between revenue officers and smugglers in such a way as to magnify the exploits of young

Hazlewood, a local landowner's son, thus conveying to us her subconscious interest in the young man.[11] This is not so much analysis as a kind of dramatic self-revelation, but a process of analysis lies behind it. When Henry Morton, the hero of *Old Mortality*, decides to leave Scotland for a soldier's life abroad but is unable to gain his uncle's consent, he is, says Scott, "perhaps not altogether displeased at the obstacles which seemed to present themselves to his leaving the neighbourhood of Tillietudlem," where his adored Edith Bellenden lives.[12] At a later stage in the book, Morton notices that his meetings with Edith are often prevented by social engagements at which Lord Evandale is present:

> and Henry could not but mark that Edith either studiously avoided speaking of the young nobleman, or did so with obvious reserve and hesitation.
>
> These symptoms, which in fact arose from the delicacy of her own feelings towards Morton himself, were misconstrued by his diffident temper, and the jealousy which they excited was fermented by the occasional observations of Jenny Dennison. This true-bred serving-damsel was, in her own person, a complete country coquette, and when she had no opportunity of teasing her own lovers, used to take some occasional opportunity to torment her young lady's.[13]

Here Scott conveys the interactions of three people by formulating their motives in terms of a set of psychological concepts which his audience also shared—the delicacy of the heroine's feelings, Morton's "diffident temper," and the set characterisation implied in the phrase "a complete country coquette." These labels imply a fairly high degree of generality behind which a process of analysis can once again be discerned. It is because of Morton's mis-apprehension of Edith's state of mind, ever so lightly and even humorously sketched in here, that the great peripety of the novel takes place—the "single and instantaneous revolution in his character" from private gentleman to liberal man of action.[14] Now Scott does not show us the transformation actually happening, or take us inside Morton's mind while it is occurring; he merely tells us that it took place and lists the reasons for it, after the fashion of an eighteenth-century historian discussing the motives and actions of a public figure. But the extraordinary thing is that we believe him; and we do so because, by means of this same rationalistic psychology, he has prepared the ground so well. In the scenes immediately preceding and immediately following the reversal, the two contrasting Henry Mortons are portrayed in action, and portrayed convincingly; there are elements in the vacillator which already prefigure Claverhouse's description of him as "a lad of fire, zeal, and education; and these knaves [the Covenanters] want but such a leader to direct their blind enthusiastic hardiness."[15]

The first seven chapters of *Waverley* work out in detail an idea which frequently occurs in Scott's works—the effect of early training and reading on mature men and women. Amy Robsart's tragedy proceeds from her preference of the glittering Leicester to the plain but honest Tressilian and "that fatal error, which ruined the happiness of her life, had its origin in the mistaken kindness that had spared her childhood the painful, but most necessary, lesson of submission and self-command." Adversity, however, causes heredity to triumph over environment, for when Amy had completed her arduous journey to Kenilworth, she prayed "for strength of body and for mental fortitude, and resolved, at the same time, to yield to no nervous impulse which might weaken either"; and yet she was able to meet the challenge because she "had naturally a mind of great power, united with a frame which her share in her father's woodland exercises had rendered uncommonly healthy."[16] In *The Abbot*, again, Roland Graeme's behaviour is the result of "a spirit naturally haughty, overbearing, and impatient" which was not "subjected to severe observance of the ancient and rigorous discipline of a feudal retainer."[17]

It is not only in *Waverley* that Scott shows himself aware of the sub-conscious mind. In *The Pirate* the two sisters Minna and Brenda Troil have semi-prophetic dreams, vaguely ominous and each in character. Minna dreams she is in a lonely cove from which she sees a mermaid emerging from a subterranean cavern, singing of "calamity and woe"; while Brenda, as befits a sociable extrovert, dreams she is asked to sing before a party of her father's friends, but that her own voice refuses to sing the cheerful songs she intends, and breaks out instead into the wild prophetic strains of the seer, Norna of Fitful Head.[18] Again, when Amy Robsart sleeps incognito in Kenilworth Castle, knowing that almost superhuman fortitude will be required of her in the days ahead, she dreams she hears the "mort," blown on a bugle at a stag's death, and sees a "scutcheon, with its usual decorations of skulls, cross-bones, and hour-glasses, surrounding a coat-of-arms, of which she could only distinguish that it was surmounted with an earl's coronet."[19] Each of these three dreams shows a union of auditory and visual imagination that is characteristic of Scott; each is called forth by a real sound in the external world—Minna's and Brenda's dreams by Norna's voice as she begins to sing a ballad outside their chamber, and Amy Robsart's by "the combined breath of many bugles, sounding not the mort but the jolly reveillé"; each is atmospheric, making its own contribution to the pattern of fatality in the novels concerned; and each exhibits Scott's simple analytical psychology in a "romantic" context.

As befits an intense visualiser, Scott likes to describe his characters as a portrait painter would paint them, often on their first appearance.[20] Sometimes he treats them iconographically,[21] or, in another style, in boldly contrasting realistic antithesis, as in the contrast between the Queen's voluptuousness and Edith's intellectual beauty in *The Talisman*. In *The Talisman*, too, the executioner is described with a painter's eye, and his features are in the Rembrandtesque shadow of "a cap of rough shag."[22] Quentin Durward manufactures two quite different pictures of Louis XI for himself out of the same features; incognito, the King looks like a money-grubbing merchant, but in his own proper person his wrinkles seem "the furrows which sagacity had worn while toiling in meditation upon the fate of nations."[23] Occasionally, Scott's pictorial treatment of character is formalised into set verbal portraits after the manner of the seventeenth-century character books, or the personages who crop up in the periodical essays of Addison and Steele; examples are the caricatures of the leading personages at the watering place of St Ronan's.[24]

Besides revealing character dramatically in action—his favourite method—Scott can display it *en passant*, by means of imagery, or he can make a person into a symbol, as when Annot Lyle becomes the emblem of innocence in *A Legend of Montrose*: the leader of the Children of the Mist, about to plunge his dirk into the body of Allan McAulay, sees and hears Annot just as his hand is on the hilt of his dagger, and he forbears to thrust.[25] In novel after novel, prophetic, gipsy-like women are associated with Destiny: Meg Merrilies in *Guy Mannering*, Ailsie Gourlay and her "witches" in *The Bride of Lammermoor*, Ulrica in *Ivanhoe*, Magdalen Graeme in *The Abbot*, Norna of Fitful Head in *The Pirate*. And there is a sense in which Edie Ochiltree (*The Antiquary*), Old Mortality himself, and Wandering Willie (*Redgauntlet*), all three of them outcast figures, are symbolic of an older and more heroic Scotland, driven into voluntary exile or abnegation by a commercially minded present.

Scott's iconographic grouping of his characters parallels, on a small scale, his method of arranging his personages in relation to the total action of a novel. In Nassau Senior's words, there is "a virtuous passive hero, who is to marry the heroine; a fierce active hero, who is to die a violent death, generally by being hanged or shot; and a fool or bore, whose duty it is to drain to the uttermost dregs one solitary fund of humour," and Senior goes on to remark that *The Abbot* is the only novel that does not contain a single one of these stock figures, while *The Antiquary* lacks the fierce Byronic-type hero, *The Bride of Lammermoor* the passive hero, and *Kenilworth*—the fool or bore.[26] Senior detested these "bores" and was quite unable to appreciate the mature, self-critical comedy behind Jonathan Oldbuck in *The Antiquary* or the mixture of love and ridicule that combined to create the Baron of Bradwardine in *Waverley*. Scott's recipe for his comic characters was borrowed from stage comedy: the reader recognises them from their characteristic "gags" whenever they appear, and builds them out of their favourite turns of phrase or psychological King Charles's heads. At their best, the bores are related to the themes and structure of the novels in which they appear, like Saddletree in *The Heart of Midlothian* or Peter Peebles in *Redgauntlet*; at their worst, they repeat their parrot cries like an advertiser's jingle, as with Sir Henry Lee in *Woodstock*. In *The Fortunes of Nigel* the main historical character, James VI of Scotland and I of England, is himself the chief "bore", and he is amongst the most successful of all Scott's creations; while Sir Mungo Malagrowther, deaf, malicious, and disillusioned, is another successful variation on the same theme. Scott has as many humerous characters as Dickens, each bustling with life—comic Highlanders, innkeepers, town land-ladies, eccentric serving men, ploughmen, decadent aristocrats, unworldly schoolmasters, vicar-of-Wakefield clergymen, malapert maidservants, and shrewish mothers, each with a telltale surname, as characteristic in its own way as Ben Jonson's Sir Politick Wouldbe or Zeal of the Land Busy. The most impressive of this group belong to the lower classes: Cuddie Headrigg, Habakkuk

Mucklewrath, Meg Dods, the Mucklebackits; as many critics have noted,[27] they rise far above the comic sphere in which they were originally conceived, to bring into British fiction the dignity, the enduring solidity, and the heroism of the very poor.

and resolute action. His plots and his reading public alike demanded that his heroines should be faced with a certain type of decision; and the attempt to give them psy- is no evidence that Scott, so much at home in a drawing room and so affectionately deferential towards *grandes dames* like Lady Abercorn,[28] was in the least concerned, intellectually speaking, with the problem of the subjection of women, or that he was distressed that the women of his own class were not assigned a more active role in the society of his day. But the fact remains that the type of novel he chose to write—the adventurous novel of action; and the type of tradition in which he felt most at home—the tradition of folk and popular art—inevitably forced him to place his womenfolk in situations of danger, or circumstances where they could aid their lovers by bold

Scott's treatment of his women characters cuts right across the divisions between "principal" and comic characters, or between upper class and lower class. There chological verisimilitude within that framework inevitably led him to portray, not the drawing-room ladies of Jane Austen or the husband-hunting social climbers of Richardson, but women who, morally speaking, ought to be free, and who, in the exceptional circumstances of the novels, act for one or two brief moments like the women of the future. The heroine may ride round the countryside and take an active part in political and family intrigues, like Die Vernon in *Rob Roy*,[29] or she may appear to dress in men's clothes, like Catherine Seyton in *The Abbot*. Parallel to the two contrasting heroes there are often two sharply differentiated types of heroine—one active, one passive.

The middle-of-the-road anxiety-ridden man of honour is often attracted to a woman of strong personality only to be rejected by her, whereupon he discovers his love for a less self-assertive girl whom he had formerly ignored. The classic instance is *Waverley*, where Flora MacIvor is at one and the same time the female political idealist (a literary forerunner of Conrad's Antonia Avellanos) and the dark-haired and dark-eyed beauty of romance, while Rose Bradwardine is the blonde chocolate-box princess of a thousand northern tales. Yet Rose is no nonentity. She is capable of taking vigorous action to save Waverley, and of nursing him during his sickness at Cairnvreckan.[30] Her courage is like Jeanie Deans's; the "domestic" upper-class beauty is as capable of heroism as the cowfeeder's daughter.[31] As we have seen, Rowena in *Ivanhoe* is naturally sweet, but superficially haughty, because of her feudal environment, whereas Rebecca is naturally haughty and commanding, but sober and realistic because of her father's training and the necessities imposed by her Jewishness; she bears herself with "a proud humility."[32] In *The Pirate* the contrast is between "the idle mirth and housewife simplicity" of Brenda and "the deep feeling and high mind of the noble-spirited Minna," as Norna puts it.[33] And in *Guy Mannering* it is between Austenish Sense and Sensibility—between Lucy Bertram, "a very pretty, a very sensible, a very affectionate girl, and I think there are few persons to whose consolatory friendship I could have recourse more freely in what are called the real evils of life," and Matilda Marchmont and Julia Mannering, who can "sympathise with distresses of sentiment as well as with actual misfor-tune."[34] In *The Bethrothed*, the two types are historically differentiated according to their social and racial characteristics; the Lucy Bertram of that novel is Rose Flammock, practical, energetic, *bourgeois*, and Flemish, and her mistress, the Lady Eveline, is herself no nonentity. Scott thus describes her in the act of tending her lover's wounds:

There was prudence, foresight, and tenderness in every
direction which she gave, and the softness of the female
sex, with their officious humanity, ever ready to assist in
alleviating human misery, seemed in her enhanced, and
rendered dignified, by the sagacity of a strong and
powerful understanding.[35]

Catherine Seyton in *The Abbot* has a vigour and spright-
liness that are more conventionally feminine; to the
accomplishments of a high-born girl she adds the vivacity
of someone like Tolstoy's Natasha, in touch with the
culture of the folk. Scott rather significantly compares her
to

some village maid, the coquette of the ring around the
Maypole

rather than to

the high-bred descendant of an ancient baron. A touch
of audacity, altogether short of effrontery, and far less
approaching to vulgarity, gave, as it were, a wildness to
all that she did.[36]

Although the practical, *bourgeois*, and anti-romantic side
of Scott approves of domesticity, he is irresistibly drawn to
depict "free," independent women. On marriage, a
woman becomes the "property" of her husband, yet even
the *hausfrau* has an active role of a sort "in the discharge of
all those quiet virtues of which home is the centre."[37]
Circumstances have put great Queens in a position to give
us a faint idea of how free women, some day, may behave:
Lindesay kneels to Mary Queen of Scots' "manliness of
spirit," not to her power or her femininity,[38] and Elizabeth
of England is shown as mixing "the strongest masculine
sense with those foibles which are chiefly supposed proper
to the female sex."[39] Indeed, of all the adjectives which
Scott applies to women, "masculine" is the most notable
and the most significant; it crops up in novel after novel.

Strong-minded, potentially free women are perhaps commoner in the lower orders than in the upper, and Scott delights to represent them—so much so that, by common consent, they are as a rule far more convincing that his "ladies." One thinks of Jenny Dennison in *Old Mortality*; or the woman who warns the fugitive Balfour of Burley about the soldiers blocking the pass,[40] or the "masculine" Maggie Mucklebackit mourning her drowned son but compelled to sell her fish as usual so that her family may eat.[41]

Scott's character-symbolism is often conveyed by stylistic means—by a heightened rhetorical language which reminds us of primitive poetry itself, or that rhythmically emotive language that Synge found in the people of the Aran Islands and Yeats in the west of Ireland. The most famous of all these flights of eloquence, Meg Merrilies' "Ride your ways" speech to Ellangowan in *Guy Mannering*,[42] has recently come under fire because the mediocre, cerebral description that precedes it converts it into "something contrived, a piece of rhetoric put into the mouth of a stagey character, not issuing from the inmost being of a real and suffering woman":[43] but even so, these flaws—if flaws they are—are slight compared to the intolerable fustian of Ulrica's death song in *Ivanhoe*[44] or Magdalen Graeme's exhortations in *The Abbot*.[45] Perhaps it is naïve to bring historical fiction to the test of our own contemporary reality: but the present writer has himself heard that great folk-singer, the late Jeannie Robertson, break into Merrilies type rhetoric which was extraordinarily convincing and moving in real life. Where Scott's prophet is of Highland stock, the influence of *Ossian* is apparent;[46] where Lowland, the natural eloquence of which the best Scottish vernacular is capable under the stimulus of strong emotion.[47] Though stylistic symbolism is most noticeable in the set speeches, its most telling strokes are often part of a vernacular interchange—"the poetry of dialect," as Lord David Cecil calls it.[48]

Exactly as in the longer poems, the unit of a Scott novel is the Scene—a fusion of sight and sound. Just as Scott makes the Meg Merrilies characters into symbols by their striking appearance and memorable speech, so too he converts buildings or objects into symbols, partly by direct description and partly by subsidiary imagery. In *St Ronan's Well*, for example, Mowbray

> handed his sister through a gallery hung with old family pictures, at the end of which was Clara's bedchamber. The moon, which at this moment looked out through a huge volume of mustering clouds that had long been boding storm, fell on the two last descendants of that ancient family, as they glided hand in hand, more like the ghosts of the deceased than like living persons, through the hall and amongst the portraits of their forefathers.[49]

This is a perfect visual presentation of one of the novel's themes—decadent aristocracy on the point of collapse. In *Old Mortality* the situation of the tower of Tillietudlem and the views which it commands are symbolic of two ways of life and two types of mind that come into conflict in the novel. Scott himself sums them up as "two prospects, the one richly cultivated and highly adorned, the other exhibiting the monotonous and dreary character of a wild and inhospitable moorland."[50] The first represents time future and the *bourgeois* world, the second—heroic values and time past. One of Scott's greatest feats of description is his rendering of the landscape of Ultima Thule—headlands and beetling cliffs projecting over battling and surging waters.[51] It is a "romantic" land-and-seascape; yet in the same novel, *The Pirate*, there is a revealing little passage that shows Scott retreating from proto-Turner and proto-Ruskin, preferring gentle variation to the sublime and the terrible, just as his gentlemanly hero prefers "civil society" to the life of adventure:

The day was delightful; there was just so much motion in the air as to disturb the little fleecy clouds which were scattered on the horizon, and by floating them occasionally over the sun, to chequer the landscape with that variety of light and shade which often gives to a bare and unenclosed scene, for the time at least, a species of charm approaching to the varieties of a cultivated and planted country. A thousand flitting hues of light and shade played over the expanse of wild moor, rocks, and inlets. . . .[52]

The whole dialectic of *Waverley* is summed up in the movement from romance to anti-romance, typified by the "progress" from a Highland landscape to a cultivated English one.[53] But even at Glennaquoich itself, the seat of the MacIvors, the conflicting themes are visually symbolised by two streams which join to form a little river. The larger stream

was placid, and even sullen in its course, wheeling in deep eddies, or sleeping in dark blue pools: but the motions of the lesser brook were rapid and furious, issuing from between precipices, like a maniac from his confinement, all foam and uproar.[54]

The streams seem to refer to the Lowland and Highland aspects of Scottish history, and at the same time to the two currents in Waverley's life and personality which draw him towards and away from "romance." Much more direct and obvious is the contrast between the trim but antiquated country house of Tully Veolan as it was before the Forty-Five and its desolation after the rebellion; the ruined building and gardens are emblems of the ruins of the Jacobite cause. Talbot's role in the complicated purchase of the Bradwardine estate and its return, renewed and restored, "in full property" to the original owner, typify the generosity that Scott wished the victors had shown to all; these acts have a false and implausible ring, for they gloss over the humiliating executions at Carlisle.[55] Sometimes Scott creates a symbolism of action that looks forward to such a novel as Dickens's *Our Mutual Friend*, with its dust heaps and Golden Dustman, or even to some of Poe's stories. At the end of *Kenilworth*, Varney, the Iago-figure, asks the miserly Tony Foster to look down into the vault at the shattered body of the Countess of Leicester:

'I see only a heap of white clothes, like a snowdrift,' said Foster. 'O God, she moves her arm!'
'Hurl something down on her—thy gold chest, Tony—it is an heavy one.'

Many years later there was discovered at Cumnor Place

a secret passage, closed by an iron door, which, opening from behind the bed in the Lady Dudley's chamber, descended to a sort of cell, in which they found an iron chest containing a quantity of gold, and a human skeleton stretched above it. The fate of Anthony Foster was now manifest. He had fled to this place of concealment, forgetting the key of the spring-lock; and being barred from escape by the means he had used for preservation of that gold for which he had sold his salvation, he had there perished miserably.[56]

Yet another type of symbolism, that of popular historical myths, marks the ending of *Woodstock*, where the incarnation of Elizabethan values, Sir Henry Lee, manages to survive long enough to bless Charles II on his Restoration.[57] In *The Monastery*, the continuity of history, the interpenetration of the present with the past, of Christian with pre-Christian culture, is symbolised by the procession of Benedictine monks that passes by the market cross of Kennaquhair—"an ancient cross of curious workmanship. . . . Close by the cross, of much greater antiquity, and scarcely less honoured, was an immensely large oak-tree, which perhaps had witnessed the worship of the Druids, ere the stately monastery to which it adjoined had raised its spires in honour of the Christian faith."[58]

We have seen that Scott has a painter's attitude to character, and likes to approach a person as a portrait-painter might a sitter. His favourite descriptive methods, whether in landscapes or interiors, are also pictorial, and he likes to establish a scene by referring to some well-known artist—Salvator Rosa,[59] Rembrandt,[60] or Raeburn,[61] for example. Sometimes we are conscious of the resemblance to painters not mentioned by Scott —Brueghel,[62] or Dutch interiors generally,[63] or Hogarth,[64] or historical painting.[65] The picturesque,[66] the Gothic,[67] the "romantic" are all pressed into service in order to produce an atmospheric *frisson*. Although the few occasions on which Scott achieves a genuinely "romantic" effect are worth noting,[68] undoubtedly his usual level is "the picturesque," as established by the descriptive writers of the previous century. Pictorial and dramatic elements fuse together, and the pageantry of the *Lays* becomes more complex in the novels: the great tournament scenes at Ashby-de-la-Zouche in *Ivanhoe*[69] spring at once to mind, but there is literally hardly a novel in which pageantry does not play a part. In book after book there are battle-scenes that equal those in *Marmion* and *The Lord of the Isles*; among the best are the Welsh attack on the castle of the Garde Douleureuse at the beginning of *The Betrothed*,[70] and the realistic depiction of Bothwell Brig and other skirmishes in *Old Mortality*.[71]

Though one should not forget the urbane complexities of the first seven chapters of *Waverley*, or the more ponderous irony of the lawcourts that suffuses the Saunders Fairford parts of *Redgauntlet*,[72] it remains true that Scott's greatest writing is to be found in his dialogue. His intention is to create the illusion of historical accuracy by presenting just enough archaic or dialectal material to persuade the reader that he is really present in a particular area at a particular time. In *Woodstock*, for example, he differentiates Sir Henry Lee—a late Elizabethan and Jacobean—from the younger royalists by peppering his conversation with Shakespearian quotations and giving him a larger fund of Wardour Street English than usual. The secretaries draw their language from religious pamphlets and the caricatures of Puritan speech purveyed by Shakespeare and other dramatists; Charles II and such roystering cavaliers as Wildrake employ terms from the Restoration drama; Everard and Alice Lee are given language much closer to that of the hero and heroine of an early nineteenth-century novel, thus providing contemporary readers with a male and female window into the unfamiliar terrain of the Civil War and Protectorate; and all the characters use imagery more frequently than did people of Scott's own day. The objection that none of this dialogue is or can be historically accurate is irrelevant to Scott's artistic purpose, as, too, is the objection that Scott employs too many "an it please yous" and "I wot nots" taken over from his medieval style. And that medieval style is itself built up from Elizabethan rather than Chaucerian expressions. In *Woodstock* there is enough near-genuine or seemingly genuine Cavalier and Puritan diction to carry the tushery quite comfortably, and the novel considered as a whole exhibits a linguistic virtuosity that few of Scott's contemporaries could equal.

No earlier novelist is so sensitive to the social implications of language. "The Two Drovers" differentiates lower-class characters according to their dialect, and depends for its stylistic effect on the interplay between Highland Scots, Lowland Scots, North-West English, the style of an English judicial summing up, and ordinary eighteenth-century narrative prose. In the novels, English countryfolk are distinguished by their dialect as effectively as Scots,[73] and various types of Scottish dialect are precisely delimited—for example, Highland Scots[74] and Aberdeenshire.[75] That the fugitive Charles II disguised as the Scots Lord Louis Kerneguy is unable to speak convincing Scots is a subtle touch; the forms he uses are those of contemporary English broadsides aping Scots speech, or the Anglo-Scots songs that bulk so large in d'Urfey's *Pills to Purge Melancholy*.[76] By linguistic means Scott can ever so lightly draw distinctions between different social classes and sub-groups of classes, as in Ch. XXXVII of *Guy Mannering*, where a group of lawyers and laymen are awaiting the reading of a will,[77] or the scene in *The Monastery* where Martin the shepherd, suddenly aware of Halbert Glendinning's innate refinement, adopts a more "town-bred" speech in an almost conscious manipulation of "language as behaviour."[78] In the same novel Sir Piercie Shafton's utterances convey at any rate the illusion of euphuism to the uninstructed reader,[79] and in *The Fortunes of Nigel* the generations are separated by their manner of speaking[80] just as they are in *Woodstock*. The Tudor-Stuart novels often make considerable use of the thieves' cant that has come down to us from that period.[81]

The style of a typical Scott novel develops the most successful devices of the narrative poems to an altogether higher level, uniting pictorial description and pageantry with realistic dialogue and non-realistic declamation. Homeric and Norse epic,[82] medieval and Renaissance epic each made their contribution, as can be seen from the deer hunt and gathering of the clans in *Waverley*;[83] and so, too, did the Gothic novel and the contemporary German tale of terror.[84] The songs and lyrics, so notable in the *Lays*, become even more important; what had been a rather tedious incidental decoration in Lewis's *The Monk* (1796) became with Scott an integral part of the total aesthetic effect. Each novel has its own kind of song, its own special pattern of *pastiche*, and these often take over the attitudes of popular song and folk balladry to link the texture with the general thematic pattern. This is most obvious in *Ivanhoe*, where the English Robin Hood balladry of the fifteenth century and later contributes to

both action and atmosphere, but it is equally true of many
other novels where allusion to ballad *motifs* has almost the
function of imagery. Thus the broadside theme of the
beguiled maid contributes to the texture of *Redgauntlet*;[85]
the stock situations of "I shall never see him more" and of
the girl rescuer in man's attire to *The Fortunes of Nigel*;[86] the
"green gown" of the forlorn seduced maiden to *The
Monastery*;[87] the "get up and bar the door" *motif* to the
stormy yet humorous scene in *The Pirate*.[88] Scott's ideal
reader was a gentleman steeped in the folk and popular
literature of both England and Scotland, who would greet
such allusions with delight; and what may seem childish
to readers brought up on the realistic novel may well have
given an intense and antiquarian pleasure to many
mature members of his original public. Scott's frequent
references to the supernatural also affect us like imagery
and form part of the texture; so, too, do the many literary
references to—amongst many others—Edgeworth,[89]
Byron,[90] Gray,[91] Coleridge,[92] Milton,[93] Shakespeare
—glanced at too often to require documentation,
Ariosto,[94] Tasso, Spenser,[95] and Burns.[96] Scott's rich
humour has always been regarded as one of his strongest
qualities. Sometimes it is a matter of situation and
dialogue, when it often derives from stage comedy. At
other times it is predominantly visual[97]—the humour of
realistic documentary[98]—or the comedy of Scottish low
life,[99] when it has a strong linguistic component. Scott's
comic Highland English[100] is a variant of the tradition of
the stage Irishman or Welshman, carrying faint implications of superiority to the poor fools that pronounce their
"d's" as "t's" and mix up the genders of personal
pronouns; and his legal comedy leans heavily on the
humour that can be extracted from technical vocabulary.

The style of a Scott novel is an amalgam of eighteenth-
century and romantic elements, with sometimes the one
predominating, and sometimes the other. His
characteristic urbanity is clearly eighteenth-century, but

his air of planless buttonholing familiarity would seem to belong more to the age of Elia—until we remember Sterne. Scott's general style, as Tillyard has pointed out, is based on Dr Johnson, Horace Walpole ("Gothic or ungothic"), Hume (and, we may add, other historians), Mrs Radcliffe, Goldsmith, Clara Reeve; and even in the more "romantic" novels

> Scott would naturally draw on Chaucer, an old ballad, Froissart, and Shakespeare in the same paragraph as readily as Horace Walpole mixed his styles in the Gothic of Strawberry Hill.[101]

But there is often a fundamental difference of kind between Scott's use of ballad and folk *motifs* and their employment by, say, Collins and Gray: if Ulrica and Norna of Fitful Head belong to the same world as "Ruin seize thee, ruthless king," Meg Merrilies and Madge Wildfire do not. The line between them may be hard to draw, but it is there nevertheless. Scott's novelty consists in the contradictoriness of the strands combining to form his texture rather than in the originality of each strand considered in isolation; in his concreteness and fondness for individual detail, which connect him with nineteenth-century realism rather than with romanticism; in his use of the very language of ordinary men and women in the Scottish novels, developed from the Scottish vernacular tradition rather than from anything in English literature; and, finally, in the loving kindness with which he renders the emotions of the very poor, as Burns and Wordsworth did in very different ways. But what is above all characteristic of Scott is not so much these new features as the co-existence of new and old in a rich and often highly satisfying blend.

REFERENCES

1. Cecil, *op. cit.*, p. 487.
2. *Wav.*, p. 5.
3. *Wav.*, pp. 173–4.
4. *Wav.*, pp. 182–3.
5. *Wav.*, p. 85.
6. *Wav.*, p. 145.
7. *The Black Dwarf*, pp. 112–4.
8. *I.*, pp. 207–8.
9. *I.*, p. 242.
10. *The Abbot*, pp. 190–1.
11. *Guy Mannering*, pp. 195–7.
12. *O.M.*, p. 54.
13. *O.M.*, p. 125.
14. *O.M.*, p. 128.
15. *O.M.*, p. 131.
16. *K.*, pp. 286, 355–6.
17. *The Abbot*, pp. 39, 30.
18. *The Pirate*, pp. 197–8.
19. *K.*, pp. 357–8.
20. *R.*, p. 30.
21. *R.*, p. 126.
22. *The Talisman*, pp. 174, 171.
23. *Quentin Durward*, p. 88.
24. *St Ronan's Well*, pp. 30–5.
25. *A Legend of Montrose*, p. 265.
26. N. W. Senior, *Essays in Fiction*, 1864, pp. 101–2.
27. Cecil, *op. cit.*, p. 285.
28. *Letters of Sir W. Scott*, 1932, II. 94–6 and *passim*.
29. *Rob Roy*, pp. 40, 146, 326–7.
30. *Wav.*, pp. 52, 235–6, 400.
31. Below, p. 91.
32. *I.*, p. 213.
33. *The Pirate*, p. 353.
34. *Guy Mannering*, p. 187.
35. *The Betrothed*, p. 229.
36. *The Abbot*, p. 252.
37. *Wav.*, p. 145.
38. *The Abbot*, p. 241.
39. *K.*, pp. 242, 370, 431.
40. *O.M.*, pp. 37, 382.
41. *A.*, pp. 284, 357.
42. *Guy Mannering*, pp. 49–50.
43. Tillyard, *op. cit.*, pp. 66–7.
44. *I.*, pp. 298–9.
45. *The Abbot*, pp. 113, 297 ff.
46. *A Legend of Montrose*, pp. 199, 205.
47. *A.*, p. 184.
48. Cecil, *op. cit.*, p. 487.
49. *St Ronan's Well*, p. 387.
50. *O.M.*, p. 108.
51. *The Pirate*, pp. 1, 27, 72 ff.
52. *Op. cit.*, p. 68.
53. *Wav.*, p. 434.
54. *Wav.*, p. 137.
55. *Wav.*, pp. 47, 388–90, 431.
56. *K.*, pp. 451–2.
57. *W.*, p. 462.
58. *M.*, p. 363.
59. *M.*, p. 218.
60. *A.*, p. 294.
61. *Wav.*, p. 444.
62. *The Betrothed*, p. 84.
63. *R.*, pp. 61 ff.
64. *R.*, p. 138.
65. *A Legend of Montrose*, pp. 251–2.
66. *Wav.*, p. 42; *A.*, pp. 146–7.
67. *The Talisman*, pp. 55–6; *The Bride of Lammermoor*, pp. 66–7.
68. "The Highland Widow," p. 453; *The Bride of Lammermoor*, pp. 180, 184.
69. *I.*, pp. 72–130.
70. *The Betrothed*, pp. 28–71.
71. *O.M.*, pp. 155–71, 286–306.
72. *R.*, pp. 8–12.
73. *R.*, p. 190; *The Fortunes of Nigel*, pp. 90–9; *K.*, p. 99.

74. *Wav.*, p. 97; *Rob Roy*, pp. 266–9; *St Ronan's Well*, pp. 89–90.
75. *A.*, p. 258.
76. *W.*, p. 245.
77. *Guy Mannering*, pp. 258–9.
78. *M.*, p. 152.
79. *M.*, pp. 122–5, 131–5.
80. *The Fortunes of Nigel*, pp. 173–5.
81. *K.*, pp. 113, 273; *The Fortunes of Nigel*, p. 199.
82. Fiske, *op. cit.*, *passim*; Batho, "Scott as Medievalist," pp. 143, 157.
83. *Wav.*, pp. 149–50.
84. *A.*, pp. 232–3, 304–5; *Quentin Durward*, pp. 395 ff.
85. *R.*, pp. 291–3.

86. *The Fortunes of Nigel*, pp. 224–5, 337 ff.
87. *M.*, p. 219.
88. *The Pirate*, pp. 41 ff.
89. *Wav.*, p. 449.
90. *The Pirate*, p. 21.
91. *I.*, p. 298.
92. *M.*, *passim*; *I.*, p. 75.
93. *W.*, pp. 305–6.
94. *I.*, p. 162.
95. *M.*, pp. 21- 30.
96. *W.*, pp. 281–2.
97. *The Pirate*, p. 114.
98. *A.*, pp. 1–16.
99. *Wav.*, pp. 198–9; *The Bride of Lammermoor*, pp. 120–30.
100. *Wav.*, p. 100.
101. Tillyard, *Essays Literary and Educational*, pp. 99, 102.

CHAPTER VI

THE HEART OF MIDLOTHIAN

The Heart of Midlothian has in this century been subjected
to more extensive critical debate than any other of Scott's
novels, and I have space to look at only some of the most
notable assessments. Robin Mayhead[1] maintains that
alone of the Waverley Novels *The Heart of Midlothian* has "a
deeply pondered and carefully worked out theme"—the
nature of justice "as it is in any age." Dorothy van Ghent
sees it as an issue between " 'verbal truth' and other kinds
of truth," which the heroine refuses to face because she
will not admit the existence of a truth higher than strict
literal accuracy.[2] Joan Pittock, on the other hand, denies
the existence of a "significant theme," but argues that the
book is Scott's best novel because it calls into play, "more
constantly and more powerfully" than elsewhere "Scott's
own national, antiquarian and legal interests"; because
the heroine "symbolises the national spirit of her race,
rank and time"; and because—by implication—it is
Scott's profoundest presentation of historical manners.[3]
David Craig, in contrast, rejects its "ordinary history" as
dead wood, claims that the theme of universal justice is
not explored in a sufficiently radical manner, and erects
"subject" as the most significant critical concept for the
novel—in this case, Presbyterianism internalised as
"intensely scrupulous conscience whose demands put
intolerable strains on the relations of family, parents and
children, person and community."[4] We can admit the
existence of both the Justice theme and Craig's "subject,"
paying due attention to each. The Justice theme is of the
same kind as those I have earlier termed "outer" themes,

but in *The Heart of Midlothian* it has become metamorphosed into an "inner" theme. The debate on the nature of Justice in general is pursued right through the book, yet it is never abstractly conceived, but is always deployed through a series of cultural oppositions—town against country, old-style Calvinism against a more moderate variety, the law of England against Scottish law, man's law against God's law (as interpreted by the Covenanters), the Covenanters' law against the law of Nature;[5] and, as Craig has noted, the most dramatic conflicts are subjectivised in the minds of Davie, Jeanie, and Effie Deans. Conscience is presented in a new way for the novel; unlike Richardson, for example. Scott sees it "in depth," as historically determined, whereas for Richardson it exists in an eternal present. Thus in *The Heart of Midlothian* the main "inner" and "outer" themes are one, but there are also subsidiary *motifs*, such as Scott's favourite preoccupation with good ends and bad means,[6] and his obsession with destiny,[7] not to speak of a whole series of both serious and comic variations on the Justice theme.

Apart altogether from the question of theme, *The Heart of Midlothian* is a very good story indeed. Our pleasure in it is that derived from old-fashioned narrative: we breathlessly follow events in time, identify ourselves with the principal figures in the tale, and experience pity, fear, laughter, and wonder as the action unfolds, just like the listeners to an ancient epic or romance. Our response, that is to say, is fundamentally a primitive one. The plot, though based on a real-life incident, the case of Helen Walker,[8] is a typical ballad plot, and a broadside one at that; it has many fairy-tale and folk elements that appeal to the deepest elements in our being—the girl who cannot tell a lie, the journey through a perilous landscape for a moral end, the beautiful set scene of the interview with the Queen, the rewards doled out to the virtuous by the benevolent Duke, the final punishment that Fate metes out to the wicked baronet. Scott does not draw solely on folk traditions for such effects; he also uses pastoral, epic (with its concentration on the national and the heroic) and tragedy, which are also modes in the high literary culture. In his handling of pastoral Scott reverses a common pattern: he begins with his heroine in a green world, propels her through a real world that is immensely varied both geographically and socially; and then returns her to another green world at the end. The tragic over-tones are seen mainly in Jeanie's predicament, for she "is in the position of Antigone and other tragic figures con-fronted by absolute alternatives, each of which has a degree of validity in theory but which are mutually exclu-sive in practice. The dramatic action takes the form of a process of bringing the heroine to acknowledge the limited validity of her choice, to learn the value of what she has more or less blindly rejected, and thereby to find place for both moral impulses in an enlarged moral vision.'"[9] The last chapter alone reads as though it contained the undigested material of still another novel about a son who kills his father, a moral tragedy which Scott had not the time, or perhaps the patience, to raise above the level of the most perfunctory melodrama.

Up to the end of the trial and Jeanie's decision to leave Edinburgh, the only blemishes are the scenes involving Jeanie and Staunton (Robertson), who behaves like one of the more tempestuous villains of a Gothic romance.[10] Some readers feel the novel begins to deteriorate as soon as Jeanie leaves Scotland—that her travels in England and her adventures with robbers and gipsies and innkeepers on the road smack too much of the rogue panoramas of, say, Smollett. But a good case can be made out for the opposite view—that the picaresque elements are in fact assimilated into the general mood and movement of the book. Thus events on the journey south are seen mainly through Jeanie's eyes, and Scott is never false to her character; she is both credible and consistent throughout.

The picaresque is solemnised by repeated allusions to *The Pilgrim's Progress*, so that Jeanie's journey is made to seem like Christiana's. It is in her interchanges with Madge Wildfire, the mad harlot once ruined by Staunton, that folk-song and folk-culture are made to carry the greatest significance and pathos. Jeanie is repeatedly called a "pilgrim"; in writing to her father from York she speaks of "her present pilgrimage"; while to Reuben Butler she writes "I keep the straight road, and just beck if ony body speaks to me ceevily."[11] Madge identifies herself with Mercy, and Jeanie with Christiana; sings Bunyan's "He that is down need fear no fall"; and interprets events in Staunton's parish in terms partly of Bunyan's allegory, partly of a folk Golden Age.[12] The Christiana parallels make Jeanie's interviews with the Stauntons, father and son, seem less ridiculous than they otherwise would; and so, too, do her firm replies to the elder Staunton, where she becomes the representative of her country, her class, and her religion. Young Staunton's hysteria is the only serious defect in the second part of the novel, but even so, his conversations with Jeanie are redeemed by a new variation on the Justice theme: "the question how far, in point of extremity" she "was entitled to save her sister's life by sacrificing that of a person who, though guilty towards the state, had done her no injury." Staunton has freely granted her the power to turn him over to justice as "the most active conspirator in the Porteous mob"; and Jeanie's inward debate on this question serves to unite the Justice theme with her role as the living symbol of Scotland herself:

> In one sense, indeed, it seemed as if denouncing the guilt of Staunton, the cause of her sister's errors and misfortunes, would have been an act of just, and even providential, retribution. But Jeanie, in the strict and severe tone of morality in which she was educated, had to consider not only the general aspect of a proposed

action, but its justness and fitness in relation to the actor, before she could be, according to her own phrase, free to enter upon it. What right had she to make a barter between the lives of Staunton and of Effie, and to sacrifice the one for the safety of the other? His guilt—that guilt for which he was amenable to the laws—was a crime against the public indeed, but it was not against her.

With this feeling there mingles a political loyalty that is surely "impure" from the standpoint of general Justice: Staunton has been guilty only according to the laws of England, not according to the real interests of Scotland:

and Jeanie felt conscious that, whoever should lodge information concerning that event, and for whatsoever purpose it might be done, it would be considered as an act of treason against the independence of Scotland . . . Yet, to part with Effie's life once more, when a word spoken might save it, pressed severely on the mind of her affectionate sister.[13]

Many readers have been dissatisfied with the whole of the last third of the novel, depicting Jeanie's return to Scotland and her happy life with Reuben. As Lukács has stressed, the book is a study of the sort of heroism of which ordinary people are capable, and it is therefore inevitable that Jeanie should return to a humdrum existence, just as Dorothea does in Goethe's *Hermann and Dorothea*, for such a return is a requirement of the epic of everyday life. Scott, however, "draws this final stage in rather too broad and philistine a detail, while Goethe, who aims at beauty of line and classical perfection, contents himself with indicating that Dorothea's heroic life is over and that she, too, must now recede into simple everyday life."[14] Nevertheless, the detail of the third part is not entirely philistine, and there are many finely imagined touches, such as old Deans's inner doctrinal struggle to rationalise his acceptance of Butler as "a placed minister of the Church of Scotland," appointed by lay patronage, which Davie had formerly abhorred. Indeed, the detail is comparable with the frame already referred to, the rural scenes near the beginning of the novel. These seem calm and placid in tempo when set beside the Porteous riots which precede them; they feature the primary cell of agrarian society, the "house and hald" of Burns's *To a Mouse*. Yet the individual farm holdings of the Butler and Deans families are not presented with any sickly idealism. Their members are real people who have to struggle to make ends meet; they are at the mercy of grasping lairds (the elder Dumbiedikes) and agrarian distress. Nor is the other green world of Argyle's western estates without its shadows—smuggling, crime and the tyranny of the Duke's factotum Knockdunder, who is as capable of illegal oppression in the interests of his master as the elder Dumbiedikes was of rack-renting poor tenants.[15] The Duke's Roseneath, too, is allegorical; it stands for the organised domains of the improving landlords, the leading class in enlightenment Scotland, where benevolence was the cardinal virtue—"the heart ay's the part ay,/ That makes us right or wrang"[16]—one of the many meanings of "heart" in the book's title. The social character of Roseneath is a slightly toned down picture of what the house of Argyll actually achieved in the course of the eighteenth century. Scott portrays with remarkable success what Eric Cregeen calls

the new landlordism of the ducal house in the years following 1737 [the very year of the main events of the novel] . . . True to its family traditions as pioneers and innovators, the house of Argyll assumed a new revolutionary role as leader of economic and social change in this setting and can be found introducing agricultural improvement in the early decades of the eighteenth century. The Dukes revolutionized the whole basis of land tenure on their estate before 1740. They built a castle at Inverary in the new Gothic style, one of the earliest examples in Britain of this fashion, laid out parks, gardens and woodlands. They built new towns and villages, piers and canals, established new industries and encouraged schemes of resettlement in the highlands to prevent emigration. One after another, with remarkable consistency, the eighteenth-century Dukes pursued this new economic policy, making Inverary the main focus of change and 'improvement' in the west highlands.[17]

Thus I was wrong when I wrote in 1965 that "the tale *degenerates* towards yet another version of pastoral." What can be said, rather, is that the final pastoral is a counter in what has, in the book's progress, become a historical fable. *The Heart of Midlothian* celebrates what was attained in the course of a long revolution, at the same time as it shows some (though insufficient) awareness of the price paid. The Cameronian Davie Deans, no longer a proud and noble enthusiast, now bears the inevitable yoke of a new age: as a calculating, improving farm-manager he advances Scotland's economic basis and the Duke's profits at the same time, while Jeanie's sphere is as narrow and apparently restricted as Natasha's at the end of *War and Peace*. One may still regret the schematism of such an ending and feel cheated that it is to a certain extent "rigged." From a historical point of view one may object that Scott's comic treatment of Knockdunder's lawless arrogance blunts our perception of the bad side of the Duke's improvements:

Tenants were often ruined by the high rents resulting from the competition for land. More than half of the small tenants who received new leases in 1737 lost them through insolvency and other causes within a decade, and in general small tenants reverted to holdings from

year to year, at the landlord's will. There was a general
and extreme instability in the occupancy of farms.[18]

And speaking absolutely one may surely claim that the
stance of benevolent landlordism was not, for Scott,
appropriate to the viewing of *contemporary* reality and the
making of implicit connexions between his story and his
own time. For most of the book Scott's point of view is that
of the peasantry. His final shift to that of the paternalist
landlords,[19] though essential to his plan, makes the novel
less universal in scope than it might otherwise have been.

Scott rounds off the novel with a moralistic conclusion
that merely serves to plaster over the summary violence of
the last chapter, proclaiming

> that the evil consequences of our crimes long survive
> their commission . . . and that the paths of virtue,
> though seldom those of worldly greatness, are always
> those of pleasantness and peace.[20]

Such a formulation is of course quite inadequate for the
real natures of Jeanie Deans and Reuben Butler as Scott
created them, even although they themselves may con-
sciously have held this belief. As often as not, the paths of
virtue lead to the madhouse and the gaol: why then deny
the truth of things with an "always," and employ a John-
sonian cadence for what is surely a most un-Johnsonian
conclusion? Dr Tillyard points out that only in *The Heart of
Midlothian* does Scott "deal genuinely" with "the conventional theme" of "rewarding virtue and punishing vice
in the correct way," and that this "is far and away his
most rigidly moral book." Tillyard's suggestion that the
final section is "an instinctive attempt to add to his choric
rendering of the genius of Scotland a second choric rendering, that of conventional pietistic morality, professed
undoubtedly by the majority of his compatriots"[21] is one
of the most interesting justifications of the last third of the
book to be made before Avrom Fleishman's study; and a

similar point is made negatively by Dorothy van Ghent when she condemns the book because the real crime is Effie's "illicit sexual indulgence . . . sex must be punished, and that is all there is to it."[22] But the main justification for the last third, however, is—as I have claimed above—on grounds of structure, genre and historical allegory.

In *The Heart of Midlothian*, background is more closely integrated with character and action than in the other novels, with the possible exception of *The Bride of Lammermoor*. In a sense Jeanie and Davie and Effie Deans really *are* the Scotland that produced them. Never before had the novel dealt so well with masses of men as in the great Porteous riot scenes at the beginning, and never before had a city been so fully or convincingly rendered—as Arnold Kettle notes, Scott's Edinburgh is far more alive, far more *real* than Fielding's London.[23] Even Jeanie's meeting with Staunton at Muschat's Cairn is vividly and concretely imagined in so far as it is seen through her eyes.[24] Donald Davie has maintained that the interview with Queen Caroline is spoilt by Argyle's mediating role, made necessary by the demands of realism—an opinion tenable only if one persists in regarding this scene as "pure romance" and only romance. But the interview is prepared by the Duke's reception of Jeanie, during which the debate on Justice is continued, and by a preliminary description of the Thames and the southern English landscape that makes the very countryside seem regal, forming a tribute to the sister kingdom quite as graceful as Dunbar's "In Praise of London." The Duke is not merely a real aristocrat, as Donald Davie stresses,[25] but another emblem of Scotland, complementary to Jeanie. He is the model of what a national statesman should be—an ideal portrait that is also true on the realistic plane; and at the same time he is the "eye" of the interview, for we share both his apprehensions as Jeanie makes a *faux pas* and his relief when her innate good sense retrieves the situation. The chapter ends with the Duke conducting Jeanie back through the avenue, "which she trode with the feeling of one who walks in her sleep"—a finely imagined touch, showing that Scott means us to believe that in her great plea Jeanie has transcended her everyday character by drawing for one brief moment on all the resources of her personality, and is now in a state of utter nervous exhaustion.[26]

In this novel the characters, with the exception of Staunton, fall into three quite different categories—types, symbolic characters and Jonsonian "humour" characters. The former display to perfection the beliefs, thought-processes and sentiments of their class and period, yet contrive to be at the same time men or women we can "inscape," to use Hopkins's expression. Reuben Butler is an excellent example of the naturalistic presentation of such a type. His social role as a moderate Calvinist is perfectly consistent with his upbringing and general traits, yet it appears subordinate to his everyday behaviour. He was a weakling at school—not nearly so strong physically as Jeanie Deans,[27] and possessed little "constitutional courage";[28] nevertheless, when forced to be the rioters' chaplain, he exhibits what can only be called moral courage. He "discharges his conscience" by first of all, despite his own terror, urging the desperadoes to spare Porteous and then, when this course has clearly failed, by demanding that Porteous be given time to prepare himself. As the instrument through which we can view the riots, Butler must necessarily possess some wavering features; as the future husband of Jeanie Deans, he must not be shown to be utterly contemptible, for this would destroy our belief in her judgment, so essential in an unimaginative heroine. A long engagement was inevitable, explains Scott, so long as Reuben was unable to secure a steady job.

Fortunately for the lovers, their passion was of no

ardent or enthusiastic cast; and a sense of duty on both sides induced them to bear with patient fortitude the protracted interval which divided them from each other.[29].

Butler is one of the triumphs of the novel; accurately imagined and completely convincing on the plane of character, he is yet beautifully dovetailed into the novel's structure and themes. In the riot sequence, for example, his moral courage emerges in relation to the debate on Justice:

> 'But what, my friends,' insisted Butler, with a generous disregard to his own safety,—'what hath constituted you his judges?' 'We are not his judges,' replied the same person; 'he has been already judged and condemned by lawful authority. We are those whom Heaven, and our righteous anger, have stirred up to execute judgment, when a corrupt government would have protected a murderer.'[30]

Meeting Staunton in the King's Park, and thinking that the young man is on his way to fight a duel, Butler does not scruple to accost him, and is not thrown into confusion when he puts his hand on his sword.[31] In the *dénouement* Butler behaves with a mature firmness and tact towards Davie Deans when the old man tells him something of which he is well aware, his own elevation to the position of a "placed minister,"[32] and towards Staunton, now Sir George, when the latter offers him a Church of England living. Once again, Butler is admirably suited to the pattern of the book, for his real character is by no means out of place in an idyll:

> 'So I leave it to you, sir, to think if I were wise, not having the wish or opportunity of spending three hundred-a-year, to covet the possession of four times that sum.'[33]

Butler is incipiently symbolic only when he comes into contact with Staunton-Robertson: then Staunton is the tempter, Butler the tempted. Staunton, in contrast, is an impure symbol—a derivative of a stock literary type, the baleful demonic tempter of Gothic fiction. Time after time he says he is "the devil"; he is described as "given up to the possession of an evil being"; and at Muschat's Cairn Jeanie really takes him for the Evil One, at least for a time. Staunton is incipiently realistic only in the Porteous scenes, as the energetic leader of an avenging mob who is gifted with the attributes of a declassed partisan *frondeur*, and towards the end of the book, as an aristocrat preparing to acknowledge his wife's "low" connexions.[34] Alexander Welsh notes that both Butler and Staunton become physically ill, and that although their afflictions have "an arbitrary physical origin," the real cause of their maladies is psychological—with Staunton it is conventional guilt, and with Butler a generalised anxiety suggesting that "an alliance with civil society and with 'reality' leaves something to be desired."[35] Butler's is, however, the *angst* of a moderate man in an age of transition; he is historically particularised, and not just a projection into the past of a universal dilemma.

Meg Murdockson is a melodramatic caricature endowed with the terrifying life of the witch-hags of our childish dreams. On the level of romantic allegory she is the evil sorceress who almost destroys the fair sinner, and who torments Christiana-Jeanie on the road: perhaps it is relevant that in the image-pattern of the book Jeanie is sometimes identified with the Lady in *Comus* as well as with Bunyan's pilgrim. Meg's daughter Madge is pure symbol, the creation, almost, of the language itself, of Scots vernacular and Scots-English folk culture. She is the singing, simpering, weeping embodiment of man's inhumanity to woman, infinitely richer and stranger than any of Wordsworth's idiot boys or deranged maidens. The Whistler, too, child of Staunton and Effie, exists almost entirely on the archetypal level. He is unsatisfactory because he seems to belong to a work with a different subject and a different tone, yet he also has his portion of life. He is endowed with a pathos that parallels Madge's—the pathos of all men who suffer and are exploited:

> 'O, ye unhappy boy,' said Jeanie, 'do ye ken what will come o' ye when ye die?' 'I shall neither feel cauld nor hunger more,' said the youth, doggedly.[36]

If the Whistler is deprived, outcast, almost gipsy, he is also the Noble Savage. Arnold Kettle sees him as a forerunner of Heathcliff,[37] and Alexander Welsh has also noted his Rousseauistic features.[38] He sets fire to the house, bounds "through the woods like a deer," and ends up as a slave in America.

> The young man had headed a conspiracy in which his inhuman master was put to death, and had then fled to the next tribe of wild Indians. He was never more heard of; and it may therefore be presumed that he lived and died after the manner of that savage people, with whom his previous habits had well fitted him to associate.[39]

The Whistler is potentially Scott's most romantic figure, in the revolutionary sense of that word; he is also among his shadowiest. Quite typically, Scott glances at his future career first with sympathy, then with disapproval—his flickering attraction towards the savage is replaced by a grimace of civilised aversion.

The historical portraits, Queen Caroline and the Duke of Argyle, are generic-emblematic individuals. Grouped in contrast like figures in a historical painting, their opposition is nevertheless also a dramatic one; they are real people who also stand for their respective nations considered from a ruling-class point of view. In the great interview scene, the Queen is negatively regal—a point emphasised by the absence of the outward trappings of

royalty, whereas the Duke, for all his position as a
suppliant, is positively regal; it is as if the spirit of van-
quished Scottish royalty, of the Scottish magnates considered as governors, has descended to him alone. He is a
King by nature, a Hero in the Carlylean sense, who is able
to read over an abstract of the case of Effie Deans

> in shorter time than can be supposed by men of
> ordinary talents; for his mind was of that acute and
> penetrating character which discovers, with the glance
> of intuition, what facts bear on the particular point that
> chances to be subjected to consideration.

Because of his choice of epithet, the Duke's immediate
comment places him in relation to the Queen's Britain as
well as to Jeanie's Scotland:

> It seems contrary to the genius of British law . . . to take
> that for granted which is not proved, or to punish with
> death for a crime which, for aught the prosecutor has
> been able to show, may not have been committed at
> all.[40]

The book contains a wealth of minor characters, "flat" in
E. M. Forster's sense of the word, who yet convince us of
their reality because of the vividness with which they are
visualised and the rich concreteness of their speech—Mrs
Dolly Dutton, the Duke's dairymaid, Mrs Glass the
London tobacconist, the lawyers at the trial, the highway-
men Jeanie meets on the road. The Judge and Coun-
sellors, standing for the new world of post-Union Scotland
and the values of what Welsh calls "civil society" are, of
course, in the most intimate relationship with the Justice
theme, and one of them, Fairbrother, behaves like a
miniature epic hero who "fought his losing cause with
courage and constancy."[41] To this group belong the
"bores" that Nassau Senior could not stand[42]—Bartoline
Saddletree and Miss Grizel Damahoy, who provide a
grotesque legal, patriotic, and moral commentary on the

trial and its aftermath, not to speak of Dumbiedikes, his housekeeper Mrs Balchristie, and the Duke's egregious Highland factotum, Captain Knockdunder. These characters are interlocked with the peripities of the action, and they also show a disposition to become fully alive. Thus Mrs Balchristie's self-interested spitefulness is merely one of the tribulations of Christiana-Jeanie; she provides the heroine with a check, if not a reversal, only to be herself checkmated when Dumbiedikes is awakened by the clatter of her victorious nagging—"like many a general, she lost the engagement by pressing her advantage too far."[43] The description of Dumbiedikes' dilapidated house exactly reflects the Laird's indolence and decayed social position.[44] And quite suddenly the "chief bore," Saddletree himself, is transformed from a caricature into an all-too-human being by a passage of essayistic analysis that shows Scott at his most urbane:

> Rochefoucault, who has torn the veil from so many foul gangrenes of the human heart, says, we find something not altogether unpleasant to us in the misfortunes of our best friends. Mr Saddletree would have been angry had any one told him that he felt pleasure in the disaster of poor Effie Deans and the disgrace of her family; and yet there is great question whether the gratification of playing the person of importance, inquiring, investigating, and laying down the law on the whole affair, did not offer, to say the least, full consolation for the pain which pure sympathy gave him on account of his wife's` kinswoman.[45]

The scene where the officer of Justice, Sharpitlaw, wins over the criminal, Ratcliffe, to become an agent of the law, is one of rounded comedy dramatically presented, and it is the ironical vitality of their vernacular Scots, so phrased as to suggest intonational patterns that can be heard in lower-class Edinburgh speech to this day, that indicates they have been raised above the plane to which their very names would appear to assign them. This scene, too, is concerned with Justice: Sharpitlaw's police morality is made to seem inferior to Ratcliffe's honour-among-thieves, which he is about to forswear.[46]

Davie, Effie, and Jeanie Deans are presented in the realistic, not the naturalistic manner. Because Davie is a heroic figure from the past who has lived on with unchanged ideas into an unheroic present, it is inevitable that his doctrinal Scots-English should seem a little inflated and occasionally prolix. To the lawyers and spectators at the trial, he appears like some antediluvian vestige; like all such creatures, he is faintly comic, largely pathetic. The element of inflation in his language, derived from the sermons of Patrick Walker[47] is not, in my opinion a blemish; small sectarian groups always use jargon, which may well have its own eloquence, to insulate them-selves from an indifferent majority. As David Craig notes, there is something slightly corrupt about Davie's reaction to Effie's predicament—"a Presbyterian conscience at the point of turning into self-righteousness and overgrown social pride,"[48] and this fits in well with the inflation of his style. Davie's problem of conscience is not whether to lie to save his daughter, but whether it is lawful for him to take part in the proceedings of a court set up by an "uncovenanted" state; his conflict is "the voice of nature . . . against the dictates of fanaticism."

'My daughter Jean may have a light in this subject that is hid frae my auld een; it is laid on her conscience, and not on mine. If she hath freedom to gang before this judicatory, and hold up her hand for this poor castaway, surely I will not say she steppeth over her bounds; and if not—' He paused in his mental argument, while a pang of unutterable anguish con-vulsed his features, yet, shaking it off, he firmly resumed the strain of his reasoning—'And IF NOT, God forbid that she should go into defection at bidding of mine! I

wunna fret the tender conscience of one bairn—no, not
to save the life of the other.'

A Roman would have devoted his daughter to death
from different feelings and motives, but not upon a more
heroic principle of duty.[49]

There is a tinge of characteristic irony in Scott's choice of
the word "heroic" here, for Davie's heroism is not
incompatible with stiffnecked pride and a consciousness
of his own moral superiority to those who did not suffer in
1679.[50] Scott continues to be ironical at Davie's expense
when he shows us how the old man becomes reconciled to
his unfanatical son-in-law; as Davie mellows, he is hardly
aware that he is accommodating himself to the new conditions.

David Craig points out that the most significant action
of the book is launched by an "accident" that is firmly
located in the relations between the old man and his two
daughters—an accident "inevitable from the nature of
these people and what has conditioned them."[51] It is
before she has left home, and Effie comes in, singing, from
a meeting with Robertson. She is just about to confide in
her sister when she has the ill-luck to utter the taboo word
"dance." "'Dance!' echoed Jeanie Deans in astonish-
ment. 'O, Effie, what could take ye to a dance?'" Davie of
course hears the wicked expression, and gives vent to a
general lecture; and it is this which constitutes the "inevitable accident" that prevents Effie from unburdening
herself. Effie has time for reflexion:

'She wad haud me nae better than the dirt below her
feet,' said Effie to herself, 'were I to confess I hae danced
wi' him four times on the green down-bye, and ance at
Maggie Macqueen's; and she'll maybe hing it owre my
head that she'll tell my father, and then she wad be
mistress and mair. But I'll no gang back there again.
I'm resolved I'll no gang back. I'll lay in a leaf of my

Bible, and that's very near as if I had made an aith, that I winna gang back.'[52]

It is clear that Effie is jealous of Jeanie, and is quite conscious of a struggle for power within the family. V. S. Pritchett[53] has said that a modern novelist would have been aware, as Scott was not, of a possible jealousy on Jeanie's part—jealousy of her prettier sister, and claims that this may well have supplied an unconscious motive for her refusal to "be mansworn." Not only is there no evidence in the text for such a suggestion, but if there were any truth in it the whole pattern of the novel would be destroyed; nevertheless, the very fact that the idea could occur to a critic of Pritchett's calibre and be taken for granted by other analysts is proof of the reality of Scott's character-drawing. Most readers feel that Effie's later metamorphosis into Lady Staunton is implausible; interestingly enough, Arnold Kettle takes a different view.[54] We may perhaps say that Effie is the type of the peasant girl whose innate spontaneity is repressed, not broken, by Presbyterianism. Folk-song and folk lore are as much a part of her as the Bible, and she has the beauty, the intelligence, and the innate delicacy to be a great lady, given the chance. If we are able to accept the possibility of a Pygmalion relationship between Staunton and Effie, then her later evolution must be termed a qualified success.

There can be no doubt about her sister Jeanie, however. She is one of the most ordinary yet most heroic characters in fiction. According to David Craig, Scott's achievement in creating Jeanie Deans is "nearer to illustrating a type from history through a kind of semipersonification,"[55] than to the creation of a real, live person. But Scott is not "illustrating from history a type"—that is, a general type, like the chaste virgin or the virtuous wife, clothed in the attributes of a particular historical period in order to give her a certain measure of concreteness, nor is Davie the generalised stern father or Effie a schematised rural coquette. It is precisely because Effie is not merely average, because she is potentially the sort of woman who in the eighteenth century could only be found in George Staunton's social class, that we find her translation into a *grande dame* and her abashment of Jeanie so inexplicably "right." The Porteous riot sequence, too, and the exposition of the Deans' ideas and upbringing by means of description and dialogue are not mere "background" or "local colour", but something quite profound; they give us the social determinants of the action.[56] Scott sets before us the angry mob without explaining it by overmuch analytical history; his method, that of the descriptive historian, enables him to distance his readers slightly, yet in spite of|that the scene is so vividly and so profoundly imagined that we sense both the discipline and the frustration of the crowd—the whole mood of a proud but subject people who identify the local authorities (the City Guard) with the distant English state.[57] Like Shakespeare and the very greatest dramatists, Scott fuses immediacy with an "alienation effect": that is the function of his historical method here, of which some have complained. Then again the main action of the first two thirds of the novel "renders concrete" the "peaks" of heroism of which an ordinary peasant girl of Jeanie's background is capable; that of the last third, which most critics dismiss as grossly inferior, has at least the function of portraying her "limits."[58]

Jeanie Deans is genetically one of those strong women whom Scott delighted in: even as a little girl, when she went to school with Reuben Butler, the boy received

> that encouragement and example from his companion, in crossing the little brooks which intersected their path, and encountering cattle, dogs, and other perils upon their journey, which the male sex in such cases usually consider it as their prerogative to extend to the weaker.[59]

She has none of the beauty or vivacity of her younger sister, but is

> short, and rather too stoutly made for her size, had grey eyes, light-coloured hair, a round good-humoured face, much tanned with the sun, and her only peculiar charm was an air of inexpressible serenity, which a good conscience, kind feelings, contented temper, and the regular discharge of all her duties, spread over her features.[60]

In her dealings with Reuben she is decidedly unromantic. Before setting out on her journey, she summons an old cottar woman and

> with a precision which, upon reflection, she herself could not help wondering at, she described and detailed the most minute steps which were to be taken, and especially such as were necessary for her father's comfort.[61]

The extremes which most concern this practical, unimaginative heroine are the extremes of a drama of conscience. David Craig has maintained that "the art with which Scott evokes" them "is not quite sensitive enough," and he quotes the "key passage" in which "Jeanie's dilemma is given most inwardly," claiming that it "is too much a sequence of ideas in an argument, too little the movement of feelings and ideas mingling in a person arguing with herself":[62]

> She remained in a state of the most agitating terror and uncertainty—afraid to communicate her thoughts freely to her father, lest she should draw forth an opinion with which she could not comply; wrung with distress on her sister's account, rendered the more acute by reflecting that the means of saving her were in her power, but were such as her conscience prohibited her from using; tossed, in short, like a vessel in an open

roadstead during a storm, and, like that vessel, resting
on one only sure cable and anchor—faith in Providence,
and a resolution to discharge her duty.

The essential characteristic of conscience, however, is that
it *is* fixed, and that it *does* prohibit; people with a strongly
inbuilt conscience must either obey it, destroy themselves,
or acquire a new conscience. Jeanie's terror and uncer-
tainty are increased because of a misunderstanding: her
father is concerned only about the legality of Jeanie giving
witness in one of the established courts, but she thinks
he is aware of her true predicament. When he says
"wherefore descend into yourself, try your ain mind with
sufficiency of soul exercise, and as you sall finally find
yourself clear to do in this matter, even so be it," Jeanie
thinks that he is leaving her free to lie if she wishes. There
is dramatic irony of the very highest sort when—still
thinking about oaths and forswearings and uncovenanted
law—he says "but if ye arena free in conscience to speak
for her in the court of judicature, follow your conscience,
Jeanie, and let God's will be done." In Jeanie's inward
response the irony is both gruesome and pathetic:

'Can this be?' said Jeanie, as the door closed on her
father—'can these be his words that I have heard, or has
the Enemy taken his voice and features to give weight
unto the counsel which causeth to perish? A sister's life,
and a father pointing out how to save it! O God deliver
me! this is a fearfu' temptation!'[63]

Scott's mastery is shown in a perfect fusion of the
humorous and the serious at one of the most solemn
moments in the book. Because of her "socially essential
determinants," Jeanie regards her entire problem in the
light of temptation, and is not in the last resort free to go
against her conscience; she is, however, free to apply that
conscience in the most heroic and most practical manner,

as is made plain by the epigraph to Ch. XXV, from *Measure for Measure*:

> I_{SAB}: Alas! what poor ability's in me
> To do him good?
> L_{UCIO}: Assay the power you have.

Once she makes her decision, Jeanie's practicality turns into its opposite while still remaining itself. "She was no heroine of romance," says Scott, but "there was something of romance in Jeanie's venturous resolution":[64] in other words, Scott is himself aware of the dialectics of her situation. The quality of her unromantic romance is expressed in the two letters she writes from York:

> For the rest, in the tenor of these epistles, Jeanie expressed, perhaps, more hopes, a firmer courage, and better spirits than she actually felt. But this was with the amiable idea of relieving her father and lover from apprehensions on her account, which she was sensible must greatly add to their other troubles. 'If they think me weel, and like to do weel,' said the poor pilgrim to herself, 'my father will be kinder to Effie, and Butler will be kinder to himself. For I ken weel that they will think mair o' me than I do o' mysell.'[65]

When Jeanie finds herself travelling with the Duke of Argyle, "and then suddenly to be left alone with him in so secluded a situation," she is overcome with awe. "A romantic heroine might have suspected and dreaded the power of her own charms; but Jeanie was too wise to let such a silly thought intrude on her mind."[66] Her morality is not quite so consistent as one might think from the trial scene, for she can stop just short of prevarication in the interests of a greater good.[67] In a recent comment, John O. Hayden has seen this inconsistency as a serious blemish.[68] But Jeanie's character, in fact, develops; Scott leads her "to a broader conception of morality, one that admits of greater human sympathy than absolute principles usually allow."[69] Or, as A. O. J. Cockshut puts it in one of the best recent studies: "she, without thought, by the sheer power of her truth and love, working on inherited tradition, guides the covenanting tradition back into a form which is viable in the new age, but more gentle and no less intense than the original form."[70] That is, the development of Jeanie's individual character proceeds in step with a development of the *social* character of Scotland. The inconsistencies—Jeanie's "little lies"—are masterly effects, essential to her "concrete presentation" as both individual and type in the Lukács sense. Right at the end of the book, when Lady Staunton gives way to "all the natural irritability of her temper" on learning of Sir George's death, "it required all Jeanie's watchful affection to prevent her from making known, in these paroxysms of affliction, much which it was of the highest importance that she should keep secret." In the dénouement, too, there occurs a comment that shows that Jeanie maintains her heroic potentialities to the end: all that is required is a situation to bring them forth. "It was in such a crisis"—the crisis of Staunton's death and Effie's hysteria—"that Jeanie's active and undaunted habits of virtuous exertion were most conspicuous."[71]

If we were to try to sum up *The Heart of Midlothian* in a single paragraph, we might perhaps term it a domestic ballad-epic in prose that explores the heroism of everyday life in relation to a series of concretely presented, historically conceived conflicts of conscience. It arouses a peculiarly satisfying aesthetic response from the way its great dramatic scenes are integrated with its total pattern. Far from being disorganised, it is "one of the most artful of Scott's romances,"[72] but its true merit comes from the way romance serves its novelistic substance: it is suffused with a remarkable sense of community; its significance is deepened by a varied and allusive texture that unfolds a whole series of recurrent folk *motifs*, descriptive images, and precisely differentiated levels of linguistic usage, such as Scots law vocabulary, Presbyterian eloquence, regional dialect, and the standard descriptive and historical prose of the later eighteenth century. Though not as tightly knit as *Waverley* or *The Bride of Lammermoor*, it is more profound than these works. It lacks the more narrowly political dimension of *Waverley*, the pervasive self-critical comedy of *The Antiquary*, the almost tragic intensity of *The Bride*, and the more conventionally epic conflicts of *Old Mortality*, but it is yet greater than all of them because in it Scott's sense of history and nationality is here more profoundly linked to one of the abiding pre-occupations of mankind—the relationship between Justice and Truth. *Redgauntlet* is technically more sophisticated, its capture of a representative turning-point in history more economical (in *The Heart of Midlothian* the "turn" is a matter of gradually revealed modifications as one generation succeeds another), but it lacks a single truly great character, in the literary sense, to integrate its theme. *The Heart of Midlothian* contains many hundreds of pages which have never been surpassed as social epic in all the annals of British fiction, and it is perhaps the highest literary achievement of that tradition which its enemies term "historicism."

REFERENCES

1. R. Mayhead, "The Heart of Midlothian: Scott as Artist," 1956, p. 277.
2. D. van Ghent, *The English Novel*, 1956, pp. 113–24.
3. J. Pittock, "The Critical Forum," 1957, p. 479.
4. D. Craig, "The Heart of Midlothian: its Religious Basis," 1958, p. 225.
5. *H.M.*, pp. 155, 162; A. Kettle, *Introduction to the English Novel*, 1953, I. 121.
6. *H.M.*, p. 166.
7. *H.M.*, p. 33.
8. *H.M.*, pp. x–xiv.
9. A. Fleishman, *The English Historical Novel*, 1971, pp. 88–9.
10. Mayhead, *op. cit.*, p. 267.

11. *H.M.*, pp. 285–7.
12. *H.M.*, pp. 318–9.
13. *H.M.*, pp. 358–60.
14. Lukács, p. 52.
15. Fleishman, pp. 96–8.
16. Burns, *Epistle to Davie*, ll. 69–70.
17. Cregeen, pp. 15, 10.
18. Cregeen, p. 14.
19. Kettle, *op. cit.*, I. 121.
20. *H.M.*, p. 538.
21. Tillyard, *Epic Strain*, p. 113.
22. van Ghent, *op. cit.*, p. 121.
23. Kettle, *op. cit.*, I. 118.
24. *H.M..*, pp. 153–4.
25. D. Davie, *The Heyday of Sir Walter Scott*, 1961, p. 14.
26. *H.M..*, pp. 390–1.
27. *H.M.*, p. 81.
28. *H.M..*, p. 136.
29. *H.M.*, p. 89.
30. *H.M.*, pp. 66–7.
31. *H.M.*, pp. 108–9.
32. *H.M.*, pp. 442 ff.
33. *H.M.*, pp. 521–2.
34. *H.M.*, pp. 63 ff., 154–6, 512 ff.
35. Welsh, pp. 146–7.
36. *H.M.*, p. 535.
37. Kettle, *op. cit.*, I. 117.
38. Welsh, p. 91.
39. *H.M.*, p. 536.
40. *H.M.*, pp. 370–1.
41. *H.M.*, p. 242.
42. Senior, *op. cit.*, pp. 100–1.
43. *H.M.*, p. 265.
44. *H.M.*, pp. 261–2.
45. *H.M.*, p. 117.

46. *H.M.*, pp. 163 ff.
47. W. S. Crockett, *The Scott Originals*, 1912, p. 230.
48. Craig, p. 170.
49. *H.M..*, p. 202.
50. *H.M.*, pp. 151–2.
51. Craig, p. 169.
52. *H.M.*, pp. 98–9.
53. V. S. Pritchett, *The Living Novel*, 1946, p. 52.
54. Kettle, *op. cit.*, I. 120.
55. Craig, p. 173.
56. G. Lukács, *Studies in European Realism*, 1950, p. 151.
57. Kettle, *op. cit.*, I. 113.
58. Lukács, *op. cit.*, p. 151.
59. *H.M..*, p. 81.
60. *H.M.*, p. 84.
61. *H.M.*, p. 258.
62. Craig, p. 173.
63. *H.M..*, pp. 204–6.
64. *H.M.*, pp. 262, 281.
65. *H.M.*, p. 288.
66. *H.M.*, p. 379.
67. *H.M.*, p. 398.
68. John O. Hayden, "Jeanie Deans: the Big Lie (and a few small ones) in *Scottish Literary Journal*, VI, No. 1 (1979), pp. 34–44.
69. Fleishman, p. 89.
70. A. O. J. Cockshut, *The Achievement of Walter Scott*, 1969, p. 191.
71. *H.M.*, p. 531.
72. Welsh, p. 134.

CHAPTER VII

SCOTT TODAY AND TOMORROW

Serious modern criticism of Scott began in the nineteen-thirties when Marxism was a potent intellectual force, and most Scott scholars have either passed through a Marxist phase themselves, or at the very least been aware of the turns and counter-turns of Marxism and neo-Marxism. Some have reacted violently against the doctrine and its method. Now Marxism is nothing if not historically based, and it may well be that when the twenty-first century passes judgment on our own it will see in the Marxism of western Europe and the English-speaking world nothing more than a facet, though an enormously important facet, of historicism in general: "the last dying kick of historicism", "a manifestation of historicism in extreme decay", to use formulas that might occur to Marxists themselves. Historically-minded critics of a whiggish or a conservative persuasion, like G. M. Young ("Scott and the Historians: the Sir Walter Scott lecture for 1946") and John Buchan in the critical parts of his 1932 biography, made contributions which do not seriously conflict with Marxist insights. Some years after Buchan Ralph Fox applied the Russian formula of "romantic realism" to Scott in *The Novel and the People*, published posthumously in 1938 (Fox had been killed in the Spanish Civil War, fighting with the International Brigade). To Fox, Scott marked a great advance on his predecessors:

He was a revolutionary innovator in one sense . . . his astonishing and fertile genius attempted to make the synthesis which the eighteenth century had failed to produce, in which the novel should unite the poetry as well as the prose of life, in which the nature-love of Rousseau should be combined with the sensibility of Sterne and the vigour and amplitude of Fielding.

Though Scott did not succeed, he was, according to Fox, "a glorious failure." His attempt miscarried for two main reasons, because he idealised the past and because "he was unable to see man as he is. His characters are not the real men and women of history, but rather his own idealizations of the early nineteenth-century English upper middle-class and the commercialized aristocracy."[1]

But few in the western world were aware of modern historicist thinking about Scott until 1951, the year of David Daiches' epoch-making article "Scott's Achievement as a Novelist" in the periodical *Nineteenth-Century Fiction*, and Arnold Kettle's chapter in his *Introduction to the Modern Novel*. Georg Lukács preceded both these critics. Though his book on the historical novel was not translated into English until 1962, it was written much earlier (1937), and his interpretation of Scott was available before 1940 in the Moscow periodical *International Literature*, an English edition of which was marketed in both Britain and America. We have it on his daughter's authority that Marx himself read and re-read Scott, and Paul Lafargue tells us that he considered *Old Mortality* a masterpiece.[2] No doubt he saw in him the same sort of paradox that so intrigued Engels when he came to examine Balzac:

Well, Balzac was politically a legitimist; his great work is a constant elegy on the irreparable decay of good society; his sympathies are with the class that is doomed to extinction. . . . That Balzac was . . . compelled to go against his own class sympathies and political prejudices, that he *saw* the necessity of the downfall of his favourite nobles and described them as people deserving no better fate; that he *saw* the real men of the future where, for the time being, they alone were to be found—that I consider one of the greatest triumphs of realism, and one of the greatest features in old Balzac.[3]

Lukács develops this hint when he comes to treat of Balzac in *Studies in European Realism*, and he analyses Scott in the same spirit. Daiches, a non-Marxist historicist who did, however, grow up in the thirties, links this contradiction to the clash between what others have termed "romantic" and "augustan" elements in Scott, affirming that Scott's best works—the Scottish novels—are anti-romantic. Scott sees that civilisation ("bourgeoisdom" to the Marxists, "civil society" to Alexander Welsh) can only be paid for by the loss of the heroism found in feudalism or clan society, or in the fanaticism of the original Cameronians. Scott, a lover of the past, was nostalgic for vanished times, yet believed in the unheroic present. The Scottish novels are repeated explorations of this paradox.

Scott's "idealizations of the early nineteenth-century upper middle class and commercialized aristocracy" occur mainly in his heroes and heroines, whose connexion with the social ideals and realities of the day has been explored by Alexander Welsh. For Welsh, Scott's fiction is projective rather than historical. "In the Waverley novels," he says, "by adhering steadfastly to the law of the land—so steadfastly that they may hardly act in any direction—the passive hero and blonde heroine demonstrate their respect for property and their fitness to possess and perpetuate the title to property for future generations."[4] Many readers would consider that the minor and lower class characters in the Scottish novels are not idealisations, but David Craig has recently challenged this view. Craig sets limits to Scott's historical accuracy, for he claims that the Cameronian peasants and preachers in *Old Mortality* are, as it were, idealisations in reverse—at once caricatures of real Puritans and projections back into the past of Scott's conservative anti-Calvinism.[5] Can the novels be "true" if so many of their characters are prejudiced distortions? Can they be genuine historical models if they contain "projective" heroes and heroines? The answer lies in Georg Lukács' insight that Scott's view is identical with the real logic of English history, which in its turn is nothing more nor less than the famous "English compromise" (he means, of course, "British").[6] Because of this, Scott pillories the extremists of both right and left, brings the moderates of both sides together, and makes the "eye" of his novels a middle of the road gentleman who is a. all times the soul of honour. A society which could demand such an ideal representative was, indeed, the unheroic result of all the heroism before Scott's day—of 1588, 1649, 1660, 1688, 1715, and 1745. Now that same real logic of British history, as it had unfolded up to Scott's time, entailed the ingestion of Scottish nationality. It is therefore hardly surprising that the *littérateurs* of the Scottish Renaissance movement of the twentieth century felt in duty bound to dismiss as so much pro-Union treachery that side of the novels which is the main source of their thematic unity.

Only two years after Daiches' article, Duncan Forbes began another important trend in Scott studies—the tracing of his links with the Scottish Enlightenment ("The Rationalism of Sir Walter Scott," *Cambridge Journal* VII, 1953, pp. 20–35), which has recently been continued by a younger generation of scholars such as P. D. Garside ("Scott and the Philosophical Historians," *Journal of the History of Ideas*, XXXVI, 1975, pp. 497–512). In the light of such research it seems no longer possible to see Scott's fictional philosophy as a simple extension of Burkean conservatism with an emphasis on "organic" community (Russel Kirk, *The Conservative Mind*, 1954). And it would be wrong to assert that because so many of Scott's ideas about history and society come from men like Adam Ferguson, Dugald Stewart, Hume, Robertson and Kames, there is therefore nothing new about his historical *vision*. Between the Enlightenment and Scott there was a profound change that was as creative in its own way as the more generally recognised transformations in the minds of Wordsworth, Coleridge and Blake. No amount of delving among these authors' eighteenth-century roots can destroy their originality, and he would be a bold critic who would claim that because the sacred river Alph recalls the archetypal beginning of *Rasselas*, therefore *Kubla Khan* is "merely" derivative of Dr Johnson. The works of the European historical imagination have their precursors, it is true—especially in Shakespeare, just as romanticism as a whole is foreshadowed in Shakespeare: but their scope and emotional colouring are new, and are due to Scott more than to any other single writer.

At about the same time as Daiches' seminal article, yet another trend in modern Scott studies, which one may dubiously label "formalism", made its appearance in articles like S. Stewart Gordon's "*Waverley* and the 'Unified Design'", *English Literary History*, XVIII, 1951. It is only within the last few years, however, that critics have begun to apply to individual poems and novels that rigorous analysis, proceeding in the first instance from the words on the page and ignoring history and background at least in the initial stages, which was pioneered in the United States by the New Critics and in Britain by the followers of I. A. Richards and F. R. Leavis. Though it may seem somewhat late in the day for this, it is still necessary to have good "new-critical" and structural studies of all the novels by persons trained to lay aside their biases and preconceptions, examining works of literature entirely on their own terms, and combining wise passiveness with wise activity. Only when we have a fairly large body of such studies will it be possible to write that full-scale modern analysis of all Scott's writings for which we have waited so long. Wise passiveness is not to be found in David Craig's 1973 article "Scott's Shortcomings as an Artist" (*Scott Bicentenary Essays*, pp. 101–14), in which allegedly typical "highlights" are examined in order to demonstrate Scott's inferiority to other novelists. Such general studies as have come from the structuralist or Leavisite camps, like Marian Cusac's *Narrative Structure in the Novels of Sir Walter Scott* (1969) and Robin Mayhead's *Walter Scott* (1973), almost inevitably stray from structure or words-on-the-page into general observations on theme, such as Mayhead's conclusion that *The Antiquary* gives us "a sombre vision underlying much extravagant comedy".

Meanwhile, and running parallel to the historicist, ideographical and formalist trends, another tendency was making itself felt—the generic and archetypal approach of Northrop Frye. As early as 1950, before Daiches' essay, Frye had put forward the main lines of his theory of romance as a genre in "The Four Forms of Prose Fiction" (*Hudson Review*, Winter 1950), best known in the form of the fourth essay in *The Anatomy of Criticism* (1957), together with hints for a quite new evaluation of Scott:

> . . . a great romancer should be examined in terms of the conventions he chose. William Morris should not be left on the side lines of prose fiction merely because the critic has not learned to take the romance form seriously. Nor, in view of what has been said about the revolutionary nature of the romance, should his choice of that form be regarded as an "escape" from his social attitude. If Scott has any claims to be a romancer, it is not good criticism to deal only with his defects as a novelist.[7]

Something of Frye's approach (particularly his observations on dark and light heroines, with *Ivanhoe* as his prime example) rubbed off on to American scholars like Cusac, Alexander Welsh and Francis Hart in the mid-sixties, but it was not until 1976, in *The Secular Scripture: a study of the*

Structure of Romance, that Frye addressed himself to Scott in any detail. There is, however, one give-away phrase, when he says that like Dickens Scott writes "on the boundary of serious fiction and romance", as if in his heart of hearts, when his conscious attention is for the moment relaxed, he does not really consider romance to be "serious fiction".

> The Waverley novels of Scott mark the absorption of realistic displacement into romance itself. Scott begins his preface to *Waverley* by outlining a number of facile romance formulas that he is *not* going to follow, and then stresses the degree of reality that his story is to have. His hero Waverley is a romantic hero, proud of his good looks and education, but, like a small-scale Don Quixote, his romantic attitude is one that confirms the supremacy of real life. He is over-impressionable, and his loves and loyalties are alike immature. If not really what Scott later called him, "a sneaking piece of imbecility", he is certainly in the central parody-romance tradition of characterization. Parody enters the structure of many other semi-romantic novels, though sometimes, as in the later novels of Dickens, it appears to be largely unconscious.[8]

The implication is that in Scott the parody is conscious, and must mean that he has more in common with Jane Austen than with Dickens. But Frye's observations on particular novels are still part of his wider argument about the romance genre as a whole and its significance for western culture, and amount to little more than a picking out of plot elements—beleaguered virgins, sometimes with miraculous powers of healing, like Rebecca in *Ivanhoe*, the lost identity of the heir, dogs or inarticulate human companions and guides, oracular prophets, outlawed societies into which the hero descends (*Rob Roy*), identical twins or at any rate close friends as mirrors of the divided self, one staying at home while the other goes off in

quest of adventure (Alan Fairford and Darsie Latimer in
Redgauntlet).

It is a pity that Frye never completed the "abandoned"
essay on the Waverley novels out of which *The Secular
Scripture* grew, and we have not yet had a full-length study
of Scott that makes use of the tension between what Frye
called "low mimetic art" and the romance genre itself. In
Scott's Novels: the plotting of historic survival (1966) Francis
Hart is obviously aware of this tension. But Hart would
not, I think, agree altogether with Frye when the latter
says that the struggles Scott describes "are within the
cycle of history, and never suggest any ultimate transcen-
ding of history." In *The Lay of the Last Minstrel*, as we have
seen, history *is* transcended in the final *Dies irae*. Hart
would have more sympathy with another of Frye's points,
that the popularity of the historical novel may be ascribed
to "the principle that there is a peculiar emotional intensity in contemplating something, including our own
earlier lives, that we know we have survived."[9] For Hart
there is a sense in which Scott is the very reverse of a
historical novelist: history is something that clogs the
individual and prevents his full development, yet the continuity of culture within time is essential for that full
development. To the individual, history is an ordeal which
it is necessary for him to pass through; and ordeals, of
course, are romance motifs. Hart sees Scott as supremely
relevant in the twentieth century, when "the best lack all
conviction, while the worst/Are full of passionate intensity." Our great problem as a species is how to survive in a
world of technological crisis, monstrous super-powers and
multi-national companies, terrorism, torture, sadistic
violence, mass starvation in the underdeveloped coun-
tries, the threat to the environment and even to all living
things. To Scott, in Hart's view, survival means an escape
from determinism, from "historical fatality", which yet
involves, within the life of time, the triumph of future over
past in a culture that preserves all that is of most worth

from former epochs. In literary structures which are like parables and fables, Scott makes love and loyalty and humane values prevail over opposing fanaticisms and abstract dogma. Significantly, the characters he most admires are Ulysses-like figures (is there a connexion with myth here?) who display in action the twin virtues of fidelity and prudence—characters like Joshua Geddes in *Redgauntlet*, Nicol Jarvie in *Rob Roy*, and Edie Ochiltree in *The Antiquary*.

Hart's passionate, learned and deeply committed book perhaps says all that can be said on Scott's relevance for the larger societies of the west. For the smaller societies, C. M. Grieve ("Hugh MacDiarmid"), though aware of Scott's "real bigness," held that Scott's positive value consisted "only" in "his objective treatment of parts of Scottish history and the partial revivication by his influence" of Flemish, Catalan, and other minority literatures. "The whole direction of Scott's line was his regret for the quite needless passing of Scottish institutions, mannerisms, etc., into English . . . Properly, Scott can only be used as a battering-ram to drive home the failure of nineteenth-century and subsequent Scottish writers to crystallize phases of Scotland's developing history in the way Scott, though only poorly, did for certain previous periods . . . Where Scott is strong is in the way in which his work reveals that for a subject nation the firm literary bulwark against the encroaching Imperialism is concentration on the national language and re-interpretation of the national history. Scott's work has real value where a stand is being made against Imperialism."[10] The suggestion in Grieve's last sentence needs considerable qualification: for example, it was of greater use to small European nations in the nineteenth century than it can ever be in Africa today. Scott can still be a living influence upon those writers who wish to come to terms with all the contradictory forces in their country's history, and it may be that it is in Eastern Europe and the

Soviet Union that his example will have most effect. One can well imagine a great Russian novelist recreating Whites and Reds, anarchists and social-revolutionaries, Trotskyists and Stalinists, kulaks and the leaders of punitive detachments, exactly as Scott tried to re-create the opposing factions of the century and a half before his time. A Russian Scott may be not only possible but necessary as the prelude to genuinely unfettered writing in his country. Whether or not he is aware of the parallel, Solzhenitsyn has attempted to fulfil this role, though one may doubt whether he has completely succeeded.

Scott's virtues are still necessary today, and nowhere more than in small nations whose identities are threatened from without and from within: there are periods when Odysseus is a better guide than Achilles or William Wallace. But I am referring principally to the play of the historical imagination upon the conflicts that have made us what we are, and to an art rooted in folk and popular traditions. If criticism leads to a new interest in Scott, helping both writers and readers to a genuinely historical understanding of their own condition, then criticism will not have been in vain: it will have helped, not hindered, invention.

REFERENCES

1. *The Novel and the People*, 1947 edn., pp. 65–6.

2. Eleanor Marx, quoted in S. S. Prawer, *Karl Marx and World Literature*, 1976, p. 396; P. Lafargue and W. Liebknecht, *Karl Marx . . . Reminiscences*, quoted in *Marx: Engels on Literature and Art*, 1952, p. 122.

3. Engels to Margaret Harkess, April 1888.

4. Welsh, p. 94.

5. Craig, pp. 185–8.

6. Lukács, p. 37.

7. *Anatomy of Criticism*, p. 305.

8. *The Secular Scripture*, pp. 101–2, 40.

9. *Ibid.*, pp. 164, 176.

10. C. M. Grieve, *Lucky Poet*, 1972 edn., p. 203.

SELECT BIBLIOGRAPHY

I. WALTER SCOTT

The general reader will find helpful information about editions of the poems and novels in I. JACK, "Sir Walter Scott: A Select Bibliography," *Sir Walter Scott*, Writers and their Work, No. 103, London 1958, though he may have to buy them second-hand or borrow them from libraries, since few works by Scott are in print at any one moment. The Penguin English Library has published editions of *Waverley* (ed. A. D. Hook) and *Old Mortality* (ed. A. Calder), both of which were in print in late 1981. At the time of writing, Everyman's Library have in print *The Abbot, The Antiquary, The Bride of Lammermoor, Guy Mannering, The Heart of Midlothian, Ivanhoe, Kenilworth, The Monastery, Quentin Durward, Redgauntlet, Rob Roy, The Talisman*, and *Waverley*, some in paperback. Signet Books have an *Ivanhoe* in print, and Panther a *Woodstock*. For the poems, the Oxford Standard Authors text is still available, ed. J. L. Robertson, and there is also a selection, containing *The Lay of the Last Minstrel, The Lady of the Lake*, and shorter poems in the Oxford Paperback English Texts (ed. T. Crawford). The serious student should go in the first instance to W. E. K. ANDERSON, "Scott", in *The English Novel: select bibliographical guides*, ed. A. E. Dyson, Oxford, 1974. He will find *The New Cambridge Bibliography of English Literature*, vol. III, 1963, henceforth cited as *C.B.E.L.*, columns 670–92, an indispensable tool. For exhaustive information about the letters printed in the Grierson edition of 1932 see J. C. CORSON, *Notes and Index to Sir Herbert Grierson's Edition of The Letters of Sir Walter Scott*, Oxford 1979.

The Dryburgh edition of Scott's poems and novels, London (A. & C. Black Limited), which consists of *Poetical Works*, ed. A. Lang, 2 vols. 1895, and *Waverley Novels*, 25 vols. 1892–4, has been used for quotations from all except the following works:

Miscellaneous Prose Works, 3 vols. Edinburgh 1848.
The Minstrelsy of the Scottish Border, ed. T. F. Henderson, 4 vols. Edinburgh 1902. Reprinted 1932.
Poems and Plays, Everyman edn., 2 vols. London 1905.
Letters of Sir W. Scott, ed. H. J. C. Grierson and others, 12 vols. London 1932.
The Journal of Sir Walter Scott, ed. W. E. K. Anderson, Oxford 1972.

II. OTHERS

The bibliography in I. JACK, *op. cit.*, gives a selection of books and articles on Scott to 1958, while J. C. CORSON in his section in the *New C.B.E.L.* already cited, updates his standard *Bibliography of Sir Walter Scott, A Classified and Annotated List of Books and Articles relating to his Life and Works 1797–1840*, Edinburgh 1943. J. T. HILLHOUSE, *The Waverley Novels and their critics* has ably summarised most English and some continental criticism of Scott up to the mid nineteen-thirties, while the period 1932–1977 has been similarly treated in JILL RUBENSTEIN, *Sir Walter Scott: a reference guide*, Boston 1978. There are also summaries in *The English Romantic Poets and Essayists: A Review of Research and Criticism*, ed. C. W. and L. H. Houtchens, 1957 and, more recently, in "The Year's Work in Scottish Literary Studies", in *Scottish Literary News*, 1970–4 and in its successor, *Scottish Literary Journal* (Supplements), from 1974. A running bibliography without evaluative comments has been published by *The Bibliotheck* in its supplement, *Annual Bibliography of Scottish Literature*, from 1970 onwards.

ADOLPHUS, J. L.: *Letters to Richard Heber*. London 1821.

ALEXANDER, J. H.: *"The Lay of the Last Minstrel": Three Essays.* Salzburg, 1978.

ANDERSON, J.: "Sir Walter Scott as Historical Novelist" (in six parts), in *Studies in Scottish Literature*, IV (1966–7), pp. 29–41, 63–78, 155–78, and V (1967–8), pp. 14–27, 83–97, 143–66.

BALL, M.: *Sir Walter Scott as a Critic of Literature*. Columbia 1907.

BALZAC, H. de: Avant-propos, *La comédie humaine*. Paris 1842.

BATHO, E. C.: *The Ettrick Shepherd*. Cambridge 1927.

———: "Scott as Medievalist," in *Sir Walter Scott Today*, ed. H. J. C. Grierson. London 1932.

BELL, A., ed.: *Scott Bicentenary Essays*. Edinburgh 1973.

BIGGINS, D.: "'Measure for Measure' and 'The Heart of Midlothian,'" in *Études Anglaises*, XIV (1961), pp. 193–205.

BOWRA, M.: *The Romantic Imagination*. London 1961.

BRADLEY, A. C.: *Oxford Lectures on Poetry*. London 1911.

BRANDL, A.: "Walter Scott über sein dichterisches Schaffen," in *Sitzungsberichte der Preussischen Akademie der Wissenschaften*, XXX (1925), pp. 356–64.

BROWN, D.: *Walter Scott and the Historical Imagination*. London 1979.

BUSHNELL, N. S.: "Walter Scott's Advent as Novelist of Manners," in *Studies in Scottish Literature*, I (1963) pp. 15–34.

CALDER, A. and J.: *Scott*. London 1969.

CARLYLE, T.: *Critical and Miscellaneous Essays*, 7 vols. London 1888.

CECIL, D.: "Sir Walter Scott," in *Atlantic Monthly*, CL (1932), pp. 277–87, 485–94.

CHILD, F. J.: *The English and Scottish Popular Ballads*, 5 vols. repr. New York 1957.

COCKBURN, H.: *Memorials of his Time*. Edinburgh 1909.

COCKSHUT, A. O. J.: *The Achievement of Walter Scott*. London 1969.

COLERIDGE, S. T.: *Biographia Epistolaria*, ed. A. Turnbull, 2 vols. London 1911.

CRAIG, D.: "The Heart of Midlothian: its Religious Basis," in *Essays in Criticism*, VIII (1958), pp. 217–25.

——: *Scottish Literature and the Scottish People 1680–1830*. London 1961.

——: "Scott's Shortcomings as an Artist", in *Scott Bicentenary Essays*, ed. A. Bell. Edinburgh 1973, pp. 101–14.

CRAWFORD, T.: "Scott as a Poet", in *Études Anglaises*, XXIV (1971), pp. 478–91.

——: "Introduction" to *Scott: Selected Poems*. Oxford 1972, pp. vii–xix.

CREGEEN, E.: See the list of abbreviated titles used in references.

CROCE, B.; *European Literature in the Nineteenth Century*, tr. D. Ainslie. London 1924.

CROCKETT, W. S.: *The Scott Originals*. Edinburgh 1912.

CURRIE, J. (ed.): *Works of Robert Burns*, 4 vols. Liverpool 1800.

DAICHES, D.: *A Critical History of English Literature*, 2 vols. London 1960.

——: Introduction to the Rinehart edition of *The Heart of Midlothian*. New York 1948.

——: "Literature and Social Mobility", in *Aspects of History and Class Consciousness*, ed. I. Mészaros. London 1971.

——: "Scott and Scotland", in *Scott Bicentenary Essays*, ed. A. Bell. Edinburgh 1973, pp. 38–60.

——: "Scott's Achievement as a Novelist," in *Literary Essays*, Edinburgh 1956, pp. 88–121.

——: "Scott's *Redgauntlet*," in *Essays Collected in Memory of James T. Hillhouse*, ed. R. C. Rathburn and M. Steinmann, Jr., Minneapolis 1958, pp. 46–59.

——: "Scott's *Waverley*: the presence of the Author," in *Nineteenth-century Scottish Fiction*, ed. I. Campbell. Manchester 1979, pp. 6–17.

——: "Sir Walter Scott and History," in *Études Anglaises*, XXIV (1971).

——: *Sir Walter Scott and his World*. London 1971.

DAVIE, D.; *The Heyday of Sir Walter Scott*. London 1961.

——: "The Poetry of Sir Walter Scott," in *Proceedings of the British Academy*, XLVII (1961), pp. 60–75.

DE QUINCEY, T.: *Collected Works*, ed. D. Masson, 14 vols. London 1888–90.

DEL LITTO, V.: "Stendhal et Walter Scott", in *Études Anglaises*, XXIV (1971), pp. 501–08.

DEVLIN, D. D.: "Scott and *Redgauntlet*," in *Review of English Literature*, IV (1963), pp. 91–103.

——: *The Author of Waverley*. London 1971.

DOBIE, M. R.: "The Development of Scott's *Minstrelsy,*" in *Transactions of the Edinburgh Bibliographical Society* II (Pt. I 1940), pp. 65–87.

DOBREE, B. (ed.): *From Anne to Victoria.* London 1937.

ELBERS, J. S.: "Isolation and Community in *The Antiquary,*" in *Nineteenth-Century Fiction,* XXVII (1973), pp. 405–23.

ELLER, R.: "Themes of Time and Art in *The Lay of the Last Minstrel",* in *Studies in Scottish Literature,* XIII (1977), pp. 43–56.

ELLIOT, W. F.: *Further Essays on Border Ballads.* Edinburgh 1910.

ELTON, O.: *Survey of English Literature 1780–1830,* 2 vols. London 1912.

FISHER, P. F.: "Providence, Fate and the Historical Imagination in Scott's *The Heart of Midlothian,*" in *Nineteenth Century Fiction,* X (1955), pp. 99–114.

FISKE, C. F.: *Epic Suggestion in the Waverley Novels.* New Haven 1940.

FLEISHMAN, A.: *The English Historical Novel.* Baltimore 1971.

FORBES, D.: "The Rationalism of Sir Walter Scott", in *Cambridge Journal,* VII (1953), pp. 20–35.

FORD, B. (ed.): *From Blake to Byron.* Harmondsworth 1957.

FORSTER, E. M.: *Aspects of the Novel.* London 1927; Harmondsworth 1962.

FOX, R.: *The Novel and the People.* London 1938; repr. 1947.

FRYE, N.: *Anatomy of Criticism.* Princeton 1957.

——: *The Secular Scripture.* Cambridge (Mass.), 1976.

GARSIDE, P. D.: "Scott, the Romantic *Past* and the Nineteenth Century", in *Review of English Studies,* XXIII (1972), pp. 147–61.

——: "Scott and the 'Philosophical Historians' ", in *Journal of the History of Ideas,* XXXVI (1975), pp. 497–512.

GORDON, R. C.: "*The Bride of Lammermoor*: a Novel of Tory Pessimism", in *Nineteenth-Century Fiction,* XII (1957), pp. 110–124.

——: *Under Which King?* Edinburgh 1969.

GORDON, R. K.: "Scott's Prose", in *Transactions of the Royal Society of Canada,* XLV (1951), pp. 13–18.

GORDON, S. Stewart: "*Waverley* and the 'Unified Design'," in *English Literary History,* XVIII (1951), pp. 107–22.

GRIERSON, H. J. C. (ed.): *Sir Walter Scott Today.* London 1932.

——: *Sir Walter Scott, Bart.* London 1938.

GRIEVE, C. M.: ("Hugh MacDiarmid"): *Lucky Poet.* London 1943; repr. 1962.

HARRY, K.: See the list of abbreviated titles used in references.

HART, F. R.: *Scott's Novels: The Plotting of Historic Survival.* Charlottesville (Virginia) 1966.

——: *The Scottish Novel: a Critical Survey.* London 1978.

HARTVEIT. L.: *Dream Within a Dream: a Thematic Approach to Scott's Vision of Fictional Reality.* Bergen 1974.

HAYDEN, J. O.: "Jeanie Deans: the Big Lie (and a few small ones)", in *Scottish Literary Journal*, VI (1), 1979, pp. 34–44.

HAZLITT, W.: *Collected Works*, ed. P. P. Howe, 21 vols. London and Toronto, 1931.

HENN, T. R.: *The Apple and the Spectroscope*. London 1951.

HILLHOUSE, J. T.: *The Waverley Novels and their Critics*. Minneapolis 1936.

HODGART, M. J. C.: *The Ballads*. London 1950.

HOOK, A. D.: "The Bride of Lammermoor: a Re-examination", in *Nineteenth-Century Fiction*, XXII (1967), pp. 111-26.

HYDE, W. J.: "Jeanie Deans and the Queen: Appearance and Reality", in *Nineteenth-Century Fiction*, XXVIII (1973), pp. 86–92.

JEFFREY, F.: *Contributions to the Edinburgh Review*, 3 vols. London 1844.

JOHNSON, E.: *Sir Walter Scott—The Great Unknown*, 2 vols. New York and London 1970.

JOHNSON, R. E.: "The Technique of Embedding in Scott's Fiction", in *Studies in Scottish Literature*, XIII (1977), pp. 63–71.

KETTLE, A.: *Introduction to the English Novel*, 2 vols. London 1951–3.

KIRK, R.: *The Conservative Mind*. London 1954.

KROEBER, K.: *Romantic Narrative Art*. Madison 1960.

LANG, A.: *Sir Walter Scott and the Border Minstrelsy*. London 1910.

LOCKHART, J. G.: *The Life of Sir Walter Scott*, 10 vols. Edinburgh 1902–3.

LUKACS, G.: *The Historical Novel* (1937), tr. H. & S. Mitchell. London 1962.

——: *Studies in European Realism* (c. 1938), tr. E. Bone. London 1950.

LYNSKEY, W.: "The Drama of the Elect and Reprobate in Scott's *Heart of Midlothian*," in *Boston University Studies in English*, IV (1960), pp. 39–48.

McCOMBIE, F.: "Scott, *Hamlet* and *The Bride of Lammermoor*", in *Essays in Criticism*, XXV (1975), pp. 419–36.

MARSHALL, W. H.: "Point of View and Structure in *The Heart of Midlothian*", in *Nineteenth-Century Fiction*, XVI (1961), pp. 257-62.

MATHIESON, WILLIE: MSS. in School of Scottish Studies Archives, University of Edinburgh.

MAYHEAD, R.: "The Heart of Midlothian: Scott as Artist," in *Essays in Criticism*, VI (1956), pp. 266–77.

——: *Walter Scott*. Cambridge 1973.

MAYO, R. D.: "The Chronology of the **Waverley** Novels," in *Publications of the Modern Language Association of America*, LXIII (1948). pp. 935–49.

MILES, J.: *Eras and Modes in English Poetry*. Berkeley and Los Angeles 1957.

MILLGATE, J.: "Guy Mannering in Edinburgh: The Evidence of the Manuscripts," in *The Library*, 5 series, XXXII (1977), pp. 238–45.

——: "'In thy rightful garb': Roles and Responsibilities in Scott's *The Abbot*," in *English Studies in Canada*, III (1977), pp. 195–206.

——: "Two versions of Regional Romance: Scott's *The Bride of Lammermoor* and Hardy's *Tess of the d'Urbervilles*", in *Studies in English Literature 1500–1900*, XVII (1977), pp. 729–38.

MITCHELL, J.: *The Walter Scott Operas*. Alabama 1977.

MONTGOMERIE, W.: *Bibliography of the Scottish Ballad Manuscripts 1730–1825*. Unpublished Ph.D. thesis. Edinburgh 1954.

——: "The Twa Corbies," in *Review of English Studies*, n.s. VI (1955), pp. 227–32.

——: "Sir Walter Scott as a Ballad Editor," in *Review of English Studies*, n.s. VII (1956), pp. 158–63.

MUIR, E.: *Scott and Scotland*. London 1936.

NEF, E.: *The Poetry of History*. New York and London 1961.

NOYES, A.: "Scott's Poetry," in *Quarterly Review*, CCXC (1952), pp. 211–25.

OLIVER, J. W.: "Scottish Poetry in the Earlier Nineteenth Century," in *Scottish Poetry: a Critical Survey*, ed. J. Kinsley, London 1955, pp. 212–30.

PARSONS, C. O.: *Witchcraft and Demonology in Scott's Fiction*. Edinburgh 1964.

PIKOULIS, J.: "Scott and *Marmion*: The Discovery of Identity", in *Modern Language Review*, LXVI (1971), pp. 738–50.

PITTOCK, J.: "The Critical Forum," in *Essays in Criticism*, VII (1957), pp. 477–9.

POPE-HENNESSY, U.: *The Laird of Abbotsford*. London 1932.

——: *Sir Walter Scott*. London 1948.

PRITCHETT, V. S.: *The Living Novel*. London 1946.

RENWICK, W. L. (ed.): *Walter Scott Lectures*. Edinburgh 1950.

RUBENSTEIN, J.: "Symbolic Characterization in *The Lady of the Lake*", in *Dalhousie Review*, LI (1971), pp. 366–73.

——: "The Dilemma of History: A Reading of Scott's *Bridal of Triermain*", in *Studies in English Literature*, XII (1972), pp. 721–34.

SCOTT, A.: *The Story of Sir Walter Scott's First Love*. Edinburgh 1896.

SENIOR, N. W.: *Essays in Fiction*. London 1864.

SHARPE, C. K.: *Letters*, ed. A. Allardyce, 2 vols. Edinburgh 1888.

SMITH, D. NICHOL: "The Poetry of Sir Walter Scott", in *University of Edinburgh Journal*, XV (1949–51), pp. 63–80.

TILLYARD, E. M. W.: *The Epic Strain in the English Novel*. London 1958.

——: "Scott's Linguistic Vagaries," in *Essays Literary and Educational*, London 1962, pp. 99–107.

TREVOR-ROPER, H.: "Sir Walter Scott and History," in *The Listener*, 19 Aug. 1971, pp. 225–32.

TWEEDSMUIR, BARON: *Sir Walter Scott*. London 1932.

VAN GHENT, D.: *The English Novel*. New York 1953.

WELSH, A.: *The Hero of the Waverley Novels*. New Haven 1963.
WITTIG, K.: *The Scottish Tradition in Literature*. Edinburgh 1958.

ADDENDA

An impressive recent contribution is Claire Lamont's edition of the 1814 *Waverley* in the light of modern textual principles, with introduction and notes (Oxford, 1981). *Scottish Literary Journal*, VII(1), 1980, prints sixteen articles on Scott; most are by younger scholars.

Among the latest books are:

ANDERSON, J.: *Sir Walter Scott and History, and other papers*. Edinburgh 1981.

FINLEY, G.: *Landscapes of Memory: Turner as Illustrator to Scott*. London 1980.

HEWITT, D. (ed.): *Scott on Himself: a Selection of the Autobiographical Writings of Walter Scott*. Edinburgh 1981.

REED, J.: *Sir Walter Scott: Landscape and Locality*. London 1980.

SCOTT, P. H.: *Walter Scott and Scotland*. Edinburgh 1981.

TULLOCH, G.: *The Language of Walter Scott: a study of his Scottish and Period Language*. London 1981.

WILSON, A. N.: *The Laird of Abbotsford*. Oxford 1980.